LET S̶̶̶̶̶̶ ̶̶̶̶̶̶
GODS LIE
COWBOYS & CTHULHU BOOK ONE

DAVID J. WEST

LOST REALMS PRESS

For Bani Kinnison

With your heart, art and smile gone

The world is a little less bright without you

Rest In Peace

CHAPTERS

For the dark places of the earth are full of the habitations of

cruelty – **PSALM 74:20**

There's gold aplenty, Forty-Niner,

In the river and on the ground

But don't dig too deep, I've found,

There's a things down there, Forty-Niner

ANONYMOUS, BALLAD OF THE 49'ER

ONE NIGHT IN MURDERER'S BAR

Porter was realistic and always felt that the sixth commandment might better have been translated as "Thou shalt not murder." Getting along in a place like Murderer's Bar without killing, even just as self-defense, was awful hard, even for a man trying to walk the straight and narrow. Maybe he didn't read the bible every day (or any day) but he did try hard to always do the right thing regardless. Life comes at you fast and plans don't always turn out how you think, but you gotta keep trying to make the best of it. That's what his Pa always said and other wiser men, too. But then, few people anywhere really believed Porter was walking that path of righteousness anyhow, and death has a way of always making another fork in the road for the living.

The current fork, Murderer's Bar, might just have been the most aptly named boomtown in the whole of the California gold rush. Cobbled together with the miners seeking their fortunes were wanted men from every foul corner of the earth, and death was a surer thing than the rising and setting of the sun.

Porter was no stranger to such, having been wanted for a murder he didn't commit in Illinois along with a few more he proudly did. Vengeance is a hard road, and once you take off down that way, you'd better keep your wits about you. Now that he was here in California, he had to be doubly alert, since a whole lot of men who would like to see him swing were working the gold fields all over the territory.

This particular boomtown was named for a sandbar on the middle fork of the American River where one Thomas Bruckner came upon a plundered camp with a firepit filled with unburnt human bones. He carved Murderers Bar into a nearby alder tree, and the name stuck.

Despite the bloody atrocities between the miners and local Indian tribes, the place was rich in gold dust and nuggets, so men persisted and populated the bar in short order. Ramshackle hovels, tiny cabins, and a few crooked boardwalks crowded along the river, acting like islands amongst a sea of treasure hunters. Numerous tents made up the rest of the town proper.

After dark here and there, a red lantern was hung, snuffed, and shortly relit awaiting the next customer. Soiled doves were a rare commodity and thus the few hereabouts made quite a killing amongst the miners. And of course, sometimes, feelings of love and jealousy couldn't help but interrupt business. A night without a few screams and shots fired would have seemed out of the ordinary.

That's why with the first cry of terror Porter hardly batted an eye. He scratched at his hound's head, and the dog named Dawg leaned into the affection. Porter had learned an hour into panning that very first day there was more money to be gained from the miners' pockets than there was from the river. No time to have a cabin framed, he opened the Round Tent Saloon as soon as he arrived not a few months gone. He drove a pack train and supplied the whiskey from Sacramento every week while his partner, Jack Smith, tended bar. It was a rough joint, but few wanted to tangle with either the proprietor or his help—including the dog. Jack was a good man in a fistfight and Bloody Creek Mary, a scar-faced native woman, didn't come by her name without reason. She had killed a gang of bandit *mestizos* that had murdered her family. A big bowie knife was never far from her hand. And Dawg was big as they come, usually with a happy-go-lucky demeanor, though if Porter gave him a cold command, the unusually silent canine could become a monster.

The second bloodcurdling wail made Port look up from counting the day's take. He puffed on his cigar and squinted toward the darkness outside. Dawg braced his legs and sniffed at the darkness. He remained mute but for the rumble of his chest.

Bloody Creek Mary stopped sweeping the hard-packed earth. "That was Susie, the blonde from Tennessee."

"You sure?" asked Porter, getting up from his chair. "Maybe Dawg and I better go check on her."

Bloody Creek Mary shook her head. "She is gone now."

Porter puffed on his cigar and looked at Jack who merely shrugged. "I still ought to check. One of these days, folks might want law and order and I can run for sheriff."

"Here?" scoffed Jack.

"I've seen other towns sprout up like this before. Yeah, I'm making a killing with the saloon and the halfway house in Buckeye Flats, but I got to try and think long term. It can't stay this wild forever, and what better way to keep the coin flowing than being the first one to shape this place up?"

Jack spit and shook his head. "This place is a flash in the pan. Besides, you're a wanted man yourself. Anybody else ever finds out you're the Mormon triggerite and you'll have a noose around your neck."

Porter nodded. "That's why I'm Mr. James B. Brown, but I could be Sheriff Brown!"

Bloody Creek Mary shushed them, saying, "Someone is coming."

Dawg padded toward the tent flap.

"We're closed, come back tomorrow," Porter barked at the emerging figures. A shuffling of feet continued closer. Ragged shapes took the form of men looming out of the darkness.

The hound made ready to spring. "Easy Dawg," commanded Porter.

A trio of Asian faces entered.

Porter recognized the men. He asked inquisitively, "Fei Buk? What's going on? Is your man wounded?"

Two Chinese men struggled inside carrying a semi-conscious man between them.

"You have trouble?" asked Jack.

Bloody Creek Mary did her part, not in helping make the men more comfortable but in stepping just outside the tent flap to see if anyone wanting to make trouble had followed them.

"Is no trouble with men," said Fei Buk, moving his hand up warily as Dawg gave him a sniff and lick across the palm.

"Is *È guǐ*," argued his companion, Wong, as he patted Dawg's head.

"What?"

"Hungry ghost," said Wong.

Fei Buk erupted a string of angry Chinese at Wong, who rattled back his own train of mean-spirited retorts.

"Come again?" interrupted Porter.

"He is sick. His gall bladder has exploded," said Fei Buk. "That's all, no other trouble. Can you help?"

Porter rubbed at his bearded chin then pulled out a knife. The sharp edge glittered in the lamplight. "I ain't never done that kinda thing, but I reckon I can try my hand if you fellers can give me some tips."

"No, no cut open." Fei Buk waved his hands back and forth. "It too late for that. Just make him comfortable. Whiskey, maybe. He is going to die. Then we take his bones back to China. We need help getting home. Want to buy a wagon and horse."

Wong looked to argue but remained silent with a glare from Fei Buk.

Porter said, "Sorry boys, I can't sell the team I've got, but I'm heading to Sacramento day after tomorrow, you can ride in the wagon with me that far, I guess."

"No time, *Gweilo*. We need sell the metal book and go, quick, quick. Now!" insisted Fei Buk.

Porter chewed at the edges of his beard. "I might have a mule and cart I can part with. But it won't carry three men, maybe a one." He cast a sidelong glance at the moaning man.

"We pay for that and get cash money too," said Fei Buk, pulling out a small bag of gold dust. "The rest with this." He dropped a heavy satchel onto the rough-hewn table. It clanked as it hit the hard wood. A long, white bone came partially tumbling out. Dawg padded closer and sniffed at it. Wong snatched it up and put it in his own sack.

Porter squinted and asked, "What the hell was that?"

"Not a man," said Fei Buk. "Not a man." He waved his hands in the air as if that might cloud the vision of what they had just witnessed.

"I could see that. It was too big. But what was it?"

Fei Buk and Wong looked sidelong at each other.

"We found something special," said Wong.

Fei Buk narrowed his gaze. "Dragon bone. We take that back to China. That not part of deal, though. We keep."

"Fine. What the hell would I do with a *dragon bone*, anyhow," said Porter, "cept maybe give it to Dawg." The big hound's tongue lolled out hungrily.

"Not dragon bone!" gasped Fei Buk.

Jack's brows raised with interest as he asked, "That other thing, the book. That what I think it is?"

"Is not gold," snapped Wong. "But still valuable."

Jack rolled his eyes.

Porter asked, "You said you wanted to sell a book?"

Fei Buk pressed for an answer. "Is valuable to you, yes? You pay now. We go on foot if we have too. But I want to buy horse or cart now."

Porter frowned. "You little bastards are rude, and I don't know what kind of a market value you think I can get you on a Chinese book. Hell, I can't even read English."

A rat-faced man named Thorne poked his head in the tent. "Evening! You boys still open?"

"We're closed, come back tomorrow," barked Porter.

"Alright, alright," said Thorne, ducking back out and vanishing into the night.

The two Chinese muttered amongst themselves a moment, signaled for the tent flaps to be closed and waited until Jack complied and drew the tent flaps shut, shrugging.

Fei Buk reached into the heavy satchel and drew out a thick, square, greenish book. "It is not Chinese but of the Old Ones. We found it when digging. Is key to another place." He demonstrated that the book could be swung open on a big corner axis point, granting a near twelve-pointed flower or star design. Engraved upon the copper plates were a curious collection of hieroglyphs, none of which could be understood by those present, so alien was their form.

Porter answered, "It ain't gold. It's just some worn out copper alloy." But he opened it and gazed over the many thin plates covered by a multitude of bizarre characters and weird drawings. He twisted it back and forth to get a good look at the central hinge point. It was like a great big rivet, smooth on one end but on the opposite side a little longer and countered, flaring to wider and slimmer sizes within fractions of an inch. He had never seen anything like it. "Puzzling."

"I said it not gold," snapped Wong.

"Any of that gold?" asked Jack.

"No," grumbled Porter.

"Still valuable to your people, yes? They like old books found in the earth, yes?" Fei Buk picked the book up off the table and handed it to Porter, who then gauged the weight in his hands. "Maybe you use key and dig for gold there yourself."

The semi-conscious man wailed loudly before passing out once again.

Jack swallowed. "Port, we need that. Could be worth a lot to the right people."

Porter played it a little cooler. "I don't know. You want just the thing's weight in cash? And you said you had to sell it tonight. You boy's steal it?"

13

Wong shook his head. "We found it up Wu Li canyon. We dug it up under a great old log and stone structure."

Jack guffawed. "Who what canyon? No such place."

Fei Buk persisted. "You call it Scorched Devil Ridge. We dug there and found it under pile of stones. But we sell and return home to China tonight."

"You found it under a marker cairn?" asked Porter.

Wong nodded.

"Someone's property marker?" asked Jack.

Porter shook his head. "Nobody but the Chinese were digging on Scorched Devil ridge. I heard that old Nisenan Indian, Ghost Horn, said it was haunted."

"Oh, I know that spot. Williamson's flume runs right by there doesn't it?"

"Yeah, it does," said Porter.

"We go now," insisted Fei Buk.

Porter scratched at his beard. "What's the rush?"

"Hungry ghosts," said Wong, voice rising into a high-pitched warble.

"You dug this up and now bad stuff is happening?"

Fei Buk and Wong looked to one another. Their companion moaned once loudly but said nothing more.

"Whiskey please, then sell you book, and we go."

Bloody Creek Mary interjected, "They fear they have disturbed the Old Ones; they fear for their lives."

The Chinese men muttered in their native tongue while the sick one moaned again.

Fei Buk pressed. "You want book or not? Is worth much to you. Only one found in whole country here abouts."

Jack and Porter chuckled at Fei Buk trying to use American slang.

"You sure you heard I'd be interested?" Porter asked.

Fei Buk nodded and looked to Bloody Creek Mary.

Bloody Creek Mary said, "They thought you would also be interested because you people collect such things."

"What do you mean, you people?" asked Jack.

"Mormons," answered Bloody Creek Mary.

"Does everybody know I'm a Mormon?" asked Porter.

"Too many for comfort, it seems," replied Jack.

Now Porter looked worried. "You all need to keep that quiet 'round here. Boggs is Alcalde of Sonoma now and would love nothing more than to string me up."

"But you are interested?" asked Fei Buk.

Porter nodded. "How much do you want?"

"How much do you have?"

Porter rubbed his forehead knowing full well he couldn't gauge the strange book relic's value. He had no clue to go on other than knowing that mummies taken from Egypt had cost the paltry sum of several hundred dollars. And this book had to be worth a whole lot more than mummies. "I can get you a mule and cart for your man along with two hundred dollars for that bag of gold dust and the book."

"Agreed."

Porter was glad he hadn't mentioned the other seventy-five dollars he had been willing to bargain up to. He had played poker a long time and didn't let his interest for the strange book show. He had been interested in such things since he was a boy growing up in Massachusetts.

"You sure this thing is real?" asked Jack.

Porter held out the book, saying, "Look at that verdigris. It's solid, and Fei Buk did not craft this. It's legitimate."

"You pay and we go now," insisted Fei Buk.

Porter doled out two hundred dollars while, without asking, Bloody Creek Mary fetched the cart and mule and had it waiting out front. They helped load the sick man into the cart and gave them a bottle of whiskey for his pain. Dawg followed them a pace and licked the dying man's hand. He reached through the slats of the cart and gave Dawg a gentle pat on the head and whispered something in Chinese ever so softly. Wong placed the sack with the dragon bone beside the dying man.

Porter pulled open a small hidden compartment on the front of the cart. "You can hide goods in there if you need to."

Fei Buk nodded gratefully and placed the wallet of money he had received from Porter inside the compartment.

Porter asked, "You in that much of a hurry? You could probably wait a few hours, a day at the most, and just bury your man here. Save you the trouble of traveling slower."

Wong shook his head. "His bones must return to Siyup. Or he will never find rest."

"Wherever that is," said Jack.

"In China."

"You can still do that after he passes in a day or so. We can make him comfortable till he goes. What is your dad-blasted rush?"

Fei Buk glanced at Wong who nodded. "We do Feng Shui and look at stars. The stars are right here soon for the Old Ones. In two days. What good for them and opens wide is very bad for us. They wake soon. We go now!"

"All right then, take care," said Porter, handing Fei Buk the reins of the mule.

The Chinese left in a hurry, the two men leading the mule since the cart could not hold the three of them.

Dawg looked wistfully after them as if he wanted to go with them.

"Look at that," said Jack. "He wants to go with them."

"No, he doesn't," said Porter. "He wants that dragon bone."

Dawg came up to Porter wagging his tail.

Porter looked at him and whispered, "Judas."

They laughed for a spell under the stars then went back inside the Round Tent.

"Awful peculiar," said Jack, picking up the strange book and turning it over in his hands, "Fei Buk saying something about the stars would be right in two days."

"Two days? So what?"

"It's going to be a night of a grand conjunction. I read about it in the almanac."

Porter argued, "I've seen the stars all my life, they're just stars, no such thing as a night when they are *right*."

"Well it seemed real enough to them."

"Just superstitions."

"I hope so."

Porter rolled his eyes in disgust then circled back to the present situation. "We can't let anyone know we have this. I need to get it to some people, have them look it over. Maybe someone else back in Salt Lake can translate it."

"And in the meantime?" asked Jack.

Porter shrugged. "Business as usual I suppose. I can meet up with some men that know more about this kind of thing than I do. I'm gonna be paying a visit to Sam Brannan about his receipts soon enough."

"And for tonight?"

Porter looked behind him at the bar. "We leave it locked up with the weekly take. It will be safe enough, I think. We'll have MacDonald on watch all night."

"Good enough."

It wasn't long after that when the night watchman, Moses MacDonald, a skinny Scot, came by and set himself up for the nightly ritual. Being that the saloon was just a tent and unable to be locked securely, Porter had taken to always having someone stand guard to keep track of his product. He used to do it himself, but it'd been enough of a hassle with the handful of thirsty miners, that he had given up and hired out a night watchman just so he could get a good night's rest.

After they bid MacDonald good night, the men went their separate ways to get some sleep. Bloody Creek Mary had her own spot too, though no one was sure exactly where that was.

ᛮ

The moon rose above the clutching canyon walls and ghostly light filtered down among the black pines. Something stalked warily between the shadows, and blood ran hot on hard-packed earth.

Something crawled inside the round tent saloon and made just enough noise for the dozing old man to twitch aware, but it was too late.

"Who's there? I got my scattergun, so you best skedaddle!"

Something stood, blacker than the night, and blocked the stars beyond the open tent flap.

Macdonald tried to bring the gun to bear but something took the wind and water from his guts.

Sharpness tore him open. Moses MacDonald somehow had enough life left in him to gasp out as his throat was slashed. A terrible, near-silent gurgle. But he did find the strength to pull the trigger on his shotgun even with horrifying hands writing over him. That warning woke the others and the murderer fled.

NO RESPECT FOR THE DECEASED

It didn't feel like he had been lying there for more than an hour to Porter. He'd just drifted off to sleep when the gunshot broke his reverie. It sounded an awful lot like MacDonald's shotgun; the report echoed across camp from that general direction, too. He didn't have time to put more than his britches and gun belt on before he raced down the moonlit path for the saloon, shirtless and barefoot.

"Get down there," he told Dawg, who raced quicker than him down to the saloon.

When he got there, Bloody Creek Mary was already sticking her head into the tent and wincing her nose in displeasure. One hand clutching that big bowie knife of hers behind her back.

Dawg came padding out of the tent.

"Well?" he asked.

"Someone killed MacDonald," she said.

"Any idea who? Anybody see anything?"

"No," she answered. "I got here first and didn't see or hear anyone."

"You didn't see anyone? Hungry ghosts maybe?" asked Jack as he strode up.

Porter frowned.

Bloody Creek Mary shook her head. "Ghosts did not do this. It was a man."

"How can you be sure?" asked Jack.

Mary pointed toward the back wall. "They took the book and a bottle of whiskey. Ghosts wouldn't do that."

"Just one bottle?" asked Jack.

Mary held up one finger.

Porter and Jack stepped inside the tent, raising their lanterns to survey the grisly scene. The copper scent of blood hung thick in the air along with stale cigar smoke. Crimson pooled around the body of MacDonald, he lay flat on his back across the table. The shotgun was still in his hands, a broken finger wedged beside the trigger where someone had tried in vain to steal the weapon from his death grip. The final blast of which had torn a few pellet holes in the far side of the tent allowing just a hint of torchlight to creep inside from the others in camp that were now roused and heading that way with bobbing orange lanterns.

Porter sniffed. "Did MacDonald smoke?"

Jack shrugged. "Not that I know of, but we could be smelling anything."

"I don't see a cigar anywhere."

"That don't mean nothing in the camp," said Jack.

Porter glanced over MacDonald. He was still warm, but his eyes were glazed over. There were no signs of footprints nor any other clue as to who had done it. As Mary had noticed, the whiskey racks were relatively untouched, even the small box of money which was sitting inside a beer cask remained untouched. The only thing really missing was the peculiar book.

"What happened up in here," asked one of the miners starting to congregate near the front flaps of the Round Tent.

Porter slammed a fist into his hand. "Those double-crossing bastards!"

"Who?" asked a miner.

"Fei Buk and his folk," answered Jack.

"Those coolie bastards!" shouted someone behind. "Let's string up all the Orientals!"

"Enough of that," growled Porter. "Only the guilty should pay. But if they think they can sell me a book then steal it back to sell again in San Francisco, they are in for a rude awakening."

Another miner piped up, "Always knew that Fei Buk was up to no good."

"Yeah," agreed a pack of miners crowding closer.

"Weren't them neither," said a man named Zeke who pushed his way forward. "They're dead, too."

"What?" Porter tilted his head, not sure he heard right.

Zeke continued, "I was heading this way from Buckeye Flat and came upon Charlie "Bart" Boles, and we found those Chinese fellers dead beside the trail just up by the forks. Someone kilt them dead jus' a little bit ago. They was all stabbed and bled out. I recognized your mule and cart and said we should be bringing it back for ya. We heard the gunshot when we was about to the top of the road above. Same killers I'd reckon."

Porter grimaced, looking at MacDonald. He had been slashed open. But it wasn't a clean cut. It was jagged and awful, more like from a beast than a blade. Blood covered the table and dirt floor beneath where he had presumably been dozing. "Jack, get a blanket and cover him up."

Zeke asked, "You want maybe me and Bart should send for the sheriff in Sonoma?"

Porter shook his head. "Not till daybreak anyway. This isn't an emergency. Till then everyone can go back on to bed. We'll get this sorted out in the morning."

"What happened?" A rather agitated, big miner named Stoney pushed forward to see.

"Someone carved up Moses MacDonald," said another.

"And the Chinese too? All three?" asked Stoney.

"All three," agreed Zeke out loud, he then turned and whispered to Porter. "Bart Boles wanted to know what was legal and such. I told him I didn't know, but reckoned we better bring 'em back into town on that cart before we just go looting their wares."

"Looting their wares?" asked Porter. "Nobody robbed them?"

"That's right. Somebody cut them up real bad but didn't take nothing that I could see. Maybe they saw my lantern coming one way and Boles coming from behind the other and they busted a hump out of there, don't know why they didn't jump me too, lessen it was maybe just a robbery because they was Chinese, or were Chinese, formerly Chinese. You know what I mean. I'm trying to respect the dead, I am."

"Nobody took anything from them?" asked Porter again.

"Not that I could see," said Zeke. "Looks like they still have all their gear and even a big wallet with some money. It was in that floorboard in the front of the cradle."

"How much?" asked Jack.

"Well," stalled Zeke, scratching his neck, "more than a hundred dollars, I'd say."

"Not a robbery," agreed Jack.

The crowd grew angrier and pressed forward, many trying to get a look at MacDonald despite Jack having covered him up with a blanket.

"Get them outta here," said Porter.

"Nothing more to see or do here, kindly leave now," said Jack. "We'll still be open tomorrow once we get everything cleaned up and figured out."

"Figured out?" asked Stoney as he pushed forward. "I heard someone say it was a knife that killed Moses, and you got that squaw of yours here always carrying her big knife. I think we know who done it. I say let's have some justice, just like we *Mountain Hounds* done for Sutter's injuns!"

That statement brought up Porter's hackles. The Mountain Hounds were an infamous gang of robbers that had murdered a number of the Indians in the area a year or so earlier just because they were Indians and got the blame for someone else killing some prospectors. That they were innocent never mattered to the Mountain Hounds. "I have it handled," said Porter gruffly. "You can all leave now."

Stoney was a brawler and mean as a bull. He was covered by short bristly brown hair over his head and face with only his lips and the tight patch of skin about his eyes and nose visible. From the appearance of his flattened nose, he'd been in plenty of fights before. "You've kept that squaw to yourself long enough, Brown. I think maybe the rest of us would like a taste. Especially if she has just killed a man."

Porter challenged him. "Well she didn't. So back off."

Stoney smirked and took a step closer, puffing on his cigar.

Dawg bared his teeth. Stoney's smirk vanished.

Porter stroked Dawg's head. "No." Dawg acknowledged his master and loped away to the rear of the saloon.

Stoney squinted his beady eyes down at Porter. He stood more than a head taller and thick as a full-grown stump.

"I said you can leave," repeated Porter.

Stoney, ever the brawler, even snorted like a bull. "Yeah? Did we interrupt something between you and that ugly squaw?"

"Why are you shirtless and shoeless, Brown?" jibed one of Stoney's rat-faced comrades.

Porter disliked the rat-faced man named Thorne. He figured he would smash his face in first after Stoney, if they didn't leave.

"You gonna sic your dog on us, Brown? Or are you gonna be a man?" taunted another one of Stoney's pack.

"Let's have some respect for the dead, and everyone go on home to bed," said Jack, trying to be as diplomatic as possible.

"Jump in a lake, Smith," snarled Thorne.

Porter chewed at the edge of his beard, he knew where this was going, and it was difficult to see how he could get out of it without a little more blood being spilt. "None of your business why I'm shirtless. Get out of my saloon," he said, straining to not let his voice crack and betray emotion.

"But I want a drink. And I think you're gonna get it for me."

"We're closed. Now go." growled Porter.

"Go? Or what?" challenged Stoney, poking a finger toward Porter's bare chest.

"Or it might get messy," Porter took off his gun belt and handed it to Jack.

Jack took the belt with one hand, but still had a firm grip on what was once MacDonald's shotgun. "Just say the word," he whispered to Porter.

Porter shook his head. "They'll go."

"All right, we're going," said Stoney softly. "We're not welcome after hours. It was an honest mistake."

His trio of toadies echoed, "An honest mistake."

Stoney made like he was turning away, but Porter had seen this kind of feint before. The big man turned to the left, winding up his massive right to come barreling back at Porter like a thunderbolt.

Porter dodged right then left, meeting the man's bearded chin with a left hook that staggered the bull and had him stepping back, blinking awake. When those eyes opened, they blazed with a hellish fury. Stoney charged like a man possessed, swinging his fists like hammers.

They struck one another like titans, crashing the tables and benches apart. It was a miracle they didn't hit poor MacDonald's table and topple the dead man over.

Dawg danced near them, barking mutely and nipping at Stoney's calves.

Porter took a good strike to the jaw, but he hit the brawler in the nose and blood poured from the man's face like a fountain. They came together, slamming at one another's ribs and bodies. Something had to break as they careened to the ground.

Porter tried to get a hold of the bigger man, to twist or break an arm, but the brawler was up with tigerish intensity and flung him away, kicking Porter in the nose. They separated for an instant then slammed together with a pummeling of fists, knee kicks, and jabs.

The brawler caught hold of Porter's long hair and yanked his head back. Porter slammed a finger into Stoney's eye and the brawler let go.

The brawler picked up the single chair in the establishment and smashed it against a table, turning it into kindling. He kept hold of a leg and swung it like a club.

Porter backed away to a table and kicked the charging man full in the chest, flinging him back toward his comrades.

His eyes nearly swollen shut, Stoney whirled about, wildly striking out. He hit one of his friends with the chair leg, knocking the man senseless.

Porter came in low, struck the brawler's kidneys, and kicked a knee out from under him before slamming fists into his jaw until Stoney dropped the chair leg.

On the floor and on his back, Stoney strained to get up but Porter pounced on top of him and continued to pummel his face.

Dawg rushed in and bit down on one of Stoney's heels, tearing the boot away, where he then savaged it.

"Yield," growled Porter.

"Never." Stoney sneered like a wild animal.

Porter clenched his teeth and smashed his fists into Stoney's face until his knuckles bled and several of the brawler's teeth came loose. Stoney ceased moving after the second hit, but Porter was fired up and struck several more times.

Dawg had torn Stoney's boot into ribbons.

"Get him outta here," Porter growled to the man's comrades. "And he owes me for the chair."

The agitated pack of Stoney's friends picked up both of their unconscious wards and carried them away, murmuring their half-hearted apologies. Only one of them, Pickax Pete, spoke, saying, "You shouldn't ought ta done that. The Mountain Hounds don't forget and forgive."

"It was an honest mistake," reminded Jack.

"Get out!" thundered Porter.

The bulk of everyone but his friends had cleared out of the Round Tent when Porter noticed one more man, an old miner with a big drooping mustache hanging above his lop-sided grin. He watched Porter with deep, penetrating eyes, examining him like a man might an insect.

"We're closed," growled Porter, irritated simply at the man's firm gaze and smirk.

The old man tipped his hat and walked out.

"You should have let me shoot Stoney," said Bloody Creek Mary, as she handed Porter a wet towel for his bloodied face.

"No, not you. I never want to give those devils an excuse on you," he said. "But Jack could've jumped in sooner."

"It was one on one. I wasn't letting anyone else get in on it," said Jack. "It was a fair fight."

"He had a chair leg."

"You had Dawg and you still won anyway. If I had helped in any way that would have been cheating and then all of his men might have jumped in and really torn the place apart."

"The place is torn apart. It's a wonder MacDonald still has a seat."

"No respect for the dead, those bastards," said Jack.

"Woowee," said Zeke. "I ain't never seen anyone give Stoney a beating like that. Have you, Boles?"

Boles agreed with a slight stutter, "No sir, never, that man is a monster. He is, he is, almost as big as the hairy wild man, he is, I told you I saw, yes sir."

Zeke interjected, "Don't start with those hairy wild man stories."

Boles paused, apparently pained that Zeke didn't like his wild man story. He continued unabated a moment later, "But Stoney, yes sir, he ain't never had a beating like that. He is probably gonna, probably gonna want to jump you now for that one, yes sir."

Porter rolled his eyes, muttering, "All I need."

"And your dog, Dawg! He done ate that man's shoe! Woowee!" shouted Zeke.

"No respect for the dead anywhere," lamented Jack.

"Is my nose crooked?" Porter asked.

"A little," said Mary, putting her hands up to adjust it.

"No." Porter pushed her hands away and did it himself. "Get me a drink." Jack handed him a whiskey bottle and Porter took a long pull. He wiped away the blood from himself and then remembered of MacDonald's passing. He pondered a long moment, collecting himself. So much had happened in such a short time that his head still reeled, but he needed answers. "You sure nothing else was taken? From any of them?"

"Nothing," affirmed Jack.

"Or from Fei Buk?"

"Not that I could tell," said Zeke.

Jack read Porter's mind. "Is there a big bone in any of their sacks?"

Zeke furrowed his brow. "A big bone?" He looked to Boles.

Boles shook his head vehemently. "There was no big bone, yes sir. Why? Big Bone?" he whispered at Zeke questioningly holding out his own hands as if sampling how big a bone could be.

"Don't worry about it," said Jack. "Forget I asked. I can't believe I asked."

Porter was puzzled. "Who else would want the book and bone? Who else even knew about them?"

"Perhaps those who worship the Old Ones," said Mary.

"Who would that be?" Porter asked her, but Mary merely shrugged.

"What bone?" Zeke looked at Boles who matched Bloody Creek Mary's shrug.

Jack said, "The Orientals did tear down that cairn. And Williamson's upper flume does go right by there."

Porter dabbed at his bloody chin. The blood dripped from his beard like a constant rain. "Yeah, but Williamson didn't erect that cairn. That thing was probably as ancient as the hills itself."

"Still couldn't hurt to go and talk to him, since Fei Buk ain't telling us anything more," said Jack.

Zeke spoke up, "Hey we brought back your mule and cart, so what is fair? And what about all the money they had? Boles and I counted out one hundred and fifty dollars."

Porter cocked an eyebrow at Zeke and the downcast Boles behind him. "Did you now? One hundred and fifty dollars, huh? But you said nothing was taken from the Chinese?"

Zeke and Boles looked sheepishly at one another.

"You can keep that fifty—twenty-five dollars apiece—if you bury them and MacDonald."

"Yes sir, but you want us to bury them Chinese, too?" drawled Boles. "What for?"

Porter stood, his bruised yet muscular body covered in sweat. "To show some damn respect to the dead, that's what for! I think I'll call what you stole from them *and me* square for that. Since I had just paid them two hundred dollars. Get it done."

"Yes sir," said Boles, leaving the sack with the offered hundred and fifty dollars behind.

Dawg coughed up a chunk of boot.

"That dog, I swear! Yes, sir," laughed Boles as Zeke tipped his hat and shoved his friend out the tent flaps.

"You're in a forgiving mood tonight, all things considered," said Jack.

"Plenty I don't know yet. And I need some answers."

"Answers will come when we look where the book was found," said Bloody Creek Mary.

"Guess we better go look at those Chinese diggings tomorrow," said Porter as he gripped his dragoon pistol. "And I still need a good night's rest."

A STIFF CORPSE

In the morning, Porter got up and dabbed some salve on his bruises. He'd bought it from a soiled dove that was expert in such things—he didn't remember her name, but she had been good at herbs and poultices. He did recall that he had asked her why she did her line of work when she was so skilled with the herbal remedies, and she replied that she enjoyed the work. He couldn't argue but remained puzzled. It wasn't more than a week or two after that that she had been killed by some John of hers, and Porter shook his head thinking that he would never understand some people.

He trotted down to the Round Tent for breakfast, Dawg scampering beside him as if he were still a puppy discovering everything for the first time. Porter could already smell the bacon Bloody Creek Mary was cooking. The sun splashed through the treetops and birds sang. It was almost hard to believe last night had been so dark and bloody. As he approached the rear of the tent, he could see the blanket-covered cart containing not only MacDonald but also the three Chinese. Dark blood leeched into the ground beneath the sagging cart.

Dawg crept up and sniffed at an exposed hand hanging outside the slats.

"Stay away from there," Porter commanded, and Dawg backed away.

Porter went into the back entrance of the tent and complained to Jack, "Why are they back there?"

"Yes, sir. Zeke and Boles swore they would take care of it in the morning. Yes, sir," he mocked.

"That ain't funny."

"Yes, it is," replied Jack with a grin. "What's the problem?"

"I didn't want to be reminded of it this morning is all. I don't want Dawg thinking he has a snack of those men." Porter sat on a bench at one of the tables. He glanced over and lamented that his favorite chair, his only chair, was smashed to bits, and he cursed softly.

"He already has a taste for thieves," said Jack, as he rubbed at Dawg's muzzle.

"They weren't thieves so far as we know. Moses was a good man."

"I'm sorry. I thought they would be here already and get them off to Boot Hill but seems you aren't the only one to sleep in," said Jack.

"I'd say I earned it last night."

"Oh, you did. I swept up a couple of Stoney's teeth this morning when I cleaned up."

"I swept them up," said Bloody Creek Mary, as she carried the pan of bacon and eggs and slipped them onto Porter's plate.

"Thanks," he grunted, before whispering a swift prayer over his food.

"She swept them up," corrected Jack, with a nod to Mary. "But I did wipe down the table as best I could. You know, for MacDonald."

"You're a hero," she quipped.

"He have any kin we should notify?" asked Porter between bites.

"MacDonald? No. But say, I did find something when Mary was sweeping."

"What?"

Jack held out a curious golden pin. It resembled a hairpin, it was small, only a couple inches long but had a wider butt end almost half the size of a penny—and a curious glyph that resembled a wavy, five-pointed star was engraved deeply upon it. It was black in the recesses and stood out clear from the golden hue of the rest of the pin.

Porter stared at it curiously. "What do you reckon that is?"

"I would think a lady's hair pin, but there ain't no ladies around here."

"Where was it? Why didn't we see it last night when we was looking for clues?" asked Porter.

Jack explained, "Because it was embedded in McDonalds left hand. He must have tore it free of his killer."

Porter spun the thing about in his own fingers, examining it from every angle. It was inexplicable, resembling nothing he had ever seen before. "You ever seen the like before Mary?"

She frowned and looked away. "Maybe some of my people have."

"You know something?" Porter cocked an eyebrow at her as he wolfed down the last bite of breakfast.

"No," she said unconvincingly. "But we could ask Ghost Horn. He might know."

Ghost Horn was a shaman. Porter had only seen the old man once but had never spoken to him. "If we could find him, would he talk to me?"

"No. But he might speak with me," she said.

"Then maybe we ought to see if we can find him after we go and take a look at Fei Buk's dig. Deal?"

Bloody Creek Mary nodded. "I'll get the horses."

"Jack, you see to it that Zeke and Boles take care of those bodies. Watch the place, Mary and I will go check out the diggings and talk to Williamson and anyone else we can to find out about this. And keep your eyes skinned for trouble, someone might come back looking for that pin."

"Will do, but hey, all that running around hunting for answers, that could be awhile. A long while."

"Yep, but I'm sure you can manage same as when I go on runs to Sacramento." He stepped out of the Round Tent and into the bright sunlight.

Mary came around the corner, already mounted on her horse. She tossed Porter the reins to his.

Jack argued, "Yeah, but then I have Bloody Creek Mary to help me when you're gone."

"I'm sure you can convince Zeke and Boles to stick around awhile. They'll make more working for us than they will panning," said Porter, as he put a foot in the stirrup and swung into the saddle. He patted the neck of his appaloosa.

Jack shrugged. "I can try and convince them of that, but they're dumb."

Porter grinned. "Like I always say, you'll manage," he called over his shoulder, as the appaloosa trotted away.

"Can I at least keep Dawg for the troublemakers?" Jack asked, trying to hold on to Dawg's collar. The big hound broke away and ran after Porter.

Porter laughed. "He stays with me."

It wasn't a terribly far ride to where Fei Buk and his kin had been digging. It was just upriver from the local claims of those who lived in Murderer's Bar. Most of the Forty-Niners wanted nothing to do with the newcomer Chinese, so they had to go further afield to stay out of trouble. They had chosen Scorched Devil Ridge because it was inhospitable and steep. It seemed that no one else wanted it... yet. Porter could relate to that, his own people, the Mormons, had claimed the Great Salt Lake Valley because they thought no one else would want it. That wasn't quite true either but close enough in this instance.

One cold stream of white water came tumbling down the gulch and half of that was taken in a flume for Williamson who had been among the first to build such contraptions. Porter recalled that each party, Williamson and the Chinese, could have argued the other was using their space and resources, but the Chinese had been amiable to ignore the flume, and Williamson was more concerned with diggings along the river bottom. So far there had been no contention. Porter wondered if that unspoken truce had remained. Could there have been a problem and thus the hurry to escape the territory? The Chinese site was far enough away that if there had been gunshots, he and the rest of Murderer's Bar might very well have not heard them. But Fei Buk didn't even have a gun, and Williamson was old and unlikely to ride up to see the flume's origin and Oriental camp unless the water wasn't flowing. As Porter rode along the trail it was plain that the flume was still going strong. The wooden box was to capacity with a swift current carrying untold gallons of water rushing by every second. Williamson's camp neared, Porter could see the faded green canvas of his tent.

"Hey, Williamson! How you doing?" Porter called out as he and Bloody Creek Mary rode closer. "It's James Brown from the Round Tent Saloon."

There was no sound but the rushing of the water from the flume as it met the river. It had its own dull roar that you would get used to and forget how loud it was once you were close by for a day or so. Every now and then Porter reminded himself that the sound of nature was loud, and we just turned it off in our own heads.

"Williamson? You around?" he called again as they trotted closer. "It's James Brown." The camp looked as if it had not been worked for a day or two. Most of the larger tools were stacked neatly beside a makeshift shed. A rockerbox was lying turned on its side near the tent. A stack of firewood was corralled next to the cookfire ring, but the ring was cold and there wasn't even the hint of a smolder from the black coals remaining within the stone circle.

Dawg sniffed a tree and promptly marked his territory.

"Knock that off, this ain't your turf." Porter dropped from the saddle and ventured to poke inside the tent.

Bloody Creek Mary remained perched in the saddle and cast a wary eye round about them.

As Porter drew back the tent flap, the smell slapped him awake. The cool mountain air and closed tent had stopped the rank stench from being worse. Williamson lay stone dead on his back, fully clothed, atop his blankets on the cot. His face was a frozen mask of horror, with mouth agape and dead white eyes open as if he had passed while screaming in terror. His fingers were clutched upward in half-curled fists as if he had been about to fight back at some unseen antagonist. Porter could see no wounds. No blood or strangulation marks. *Williamson was mighty old*, Porter thought, *perhaps he simply had an aneurism or heart attack.* But that look on Williamson's face, it was pure terror forever chiseled into his wrinkled, marble-like visage.

Dawg stuck his nose inside and whined, then scampered away.

"He's dead," Porter said as he stepped out of the tent. "Looks like he might have just had a heart attack and passed on," he continued before Bloody Creek Mary could ask what had happened, but she remained silent and stoic as ever. "But it is strange. As if he was crying out in terror."

"When death comes is anyone ready?" she asked.

He shook his head. "Few enough, I reckon."

He listened to the dull roar of the river a moment before he mounted his horse and continued his train of thought out loud. "I can't see that Fei Buk had anything to do with it, but maybe if he found Williamson like that, he thought he better clear out before anyone like Stoney and the Mountain

Hounds decided he might have been responsible. Not a real forgiving lot around here for his kind."

"We still go to their camp?" she asked.

"Yeah, we're most of the way there anyway," agreed Porter, kicking his appaloosa's flanks to mount up the steep path. Dawg happily raced beside them.

They followed the trail alongside the flume for some time, gaining a good bit of altitude. Despite the day wearing on, the chill in the air was palpable, and their breath came out in clouds for the first time of the season. Winter might be early.

The Chinese camp was abandoned. Clearly Fei Buk, Wong, and the other burst gall-bladder man that Porter did not know the name of, had not left anything of value. *Why would they?* he asked himself. What did he really expect to find up here? There was bare patch of ground where their tent had been and a stone circle denoting their camp and cookfire. In another winter, no one would be able to tell anyone had lived here for a spring and summer. Given time, this place would look just like it did before gold was discovered.

Porter dismounted and strode about the campsite. He kicked at a small smooth river stone and pondered a long moment then looked toward the still rushing flume. A few trails of hardpacked ground ran like a crossroads from the area. One went further into the woods to the left where they must have built a privy, and another trail went to the right where they had their diggings. Porter followed that path and glanced over the section of mountain beside the stream that the Chinese had cleared. Soon enough, no one would be able to tell they had dug there either.

Dawg ran back and forth crossing the stream and racing up the other side as if trying to catch a scent that was long gone.

Porter strode back to where Bloody Creek Mary remained on her horse. "Don't make sense," he said. "There are no answers to anything up here."

"That's because the questions don't come from here," she replied.

"What do you mean?"

"They weren't really digging here. That ground too grown over," she pointed out. "No one has dug there for weeks."

Porter glanced back and saw she was right. Small tufts of grass and dandelions were sprouting up on the hillside where they had done some digging, but not at least for a couple weeks.

"Now you're talking," said Porter. "But where were they digging then?"

Bloody Creek Mary gave as close to a smile as she ever did, kicked heels to her horse, and followed the trail and flume farther up the ridgeline. "To wherever that stone marker was."

Porter laughed to himself. "You're something all right. Come on, Dawg," he said to his hound as he mounted his horse and trotted after her, the dog at his heels.

They came to a spot where the ridge continued up like a razorback, but a trail was dug out across it at least six feet wide. The flume continued with the creek farther up, staying on the opposite side of the ridgeline. The passage opened to a bowl-like dug-out. It would have been invisible to anyone far below on the river. A stand of trees remained like a shield wall blocking the view but to anyone who stood where both Porter and Mary were, far above the river. Porter recognized some of the sand bars far below. The wide spot had a furrow of piled earth where the Chinese must surely have been digging into the fresh soil. Why? What was here? Dragon bones? Copper books? Golden pins with etchings of stars? It was free of most rock and did not look like an ideal spot to dig for gold.

Dawg growled.

"What is it boy?"

They were not alone.

THE DARK AND BLOODY GROUND

A handful of Indians were at work upon the edge of the steep embankment trying to bury something. Only one had a crude spade, the others were using sticks and baskets, even their hands, as they pulled the reddish soil over a gouge in the hillside.

"What the hell is this?" barked Porter.

Mary translated quickly, because the Indians, while not appearing armed, outnumbered them by five to one.

Two continued in their efforts to bury something, while several paused, staring in surprise. Two more stood defiant, now facing Porter and Mary.

One answered in a stern tongue that Porter had no way of understanding.

"We should go," said Mary. "They say we are intruding on a sacred burial ground."

"Hogwash. I know enough about the local tribes to know they don't do that. They bury their folk in open air travois or cremate them, they don't do this, digging like dogs burying a bone. 'Sides, the Chinese were digging here. What's going on?"

The largest of the Indians, a strong young man, stepped forward. He cast down his shovel and shouted something at Porter.

"Uh huh." Porter moved a hand closer to his six-gun. "Mary, what did he say?"

Mary was walking her horse back and away. "Slow Badger says we must leave. They say this spot is dedicated to the deep old gods."

The brave known as Slow Badger started toward them, unarmed yet defiant and with a determined look upon his face.

"Slow Badger, huh?" asked Porter. He reached into his pocket and produced the golden hairpin with the strange design on it and held it out so Slow Badger could see it. "You recognize this?"

The strapping young brave paused and gasped before looking back accusingly at the other one who had stood staring at them.

"Looks like we found our culprit." Porter drew his gun. "What's his name? I ain't gonna hang a man without knowing his name."

Mary cautioned, "They aren't going to let us hang him."

Porter gritted his teeth and pulled on the reins with his free hand as his horse bristled at the uncomfortable tension.

"You tell the rest of 'em to back off. I only want the murderer of MacDonald and the Chinese. I suspect it's the same man."

"It's all of them," said Mary, shaking her head.

Porter glanced warily at Mary. "Why didn't you tell me that before?"

Slow Badger called out something and pointed at the fresh turned earth. He backed toward the others with hands raised. He spoke a lot more calmly now that Porter had both drawn his gun and shown him the pin.

"I would not get off your horse yet," Mary said softly. "Slow Badger said he will submit Prairie Dog to you for the white man's justice, but they must cover the dead gods first."

"That brave just had you say as close to a mouthful as you ever do. You paraphrasing him good or what?"

"I'm making his words come to sense in English," she said sourly. "He also wants the pin of protection back."

"Fat chance," growled Porter. "I ain't giving up evidence."

"They may fight us for it," whispered Mary. "It means more to them than you can understand."

Just as she had said, Slow Badger warily watched Porter as he and the others continued burying whatever was just beneath the surface. Slow Badger called out once again, as if still entreating for the return of the golden pin.

Porter watched, curious at what was there in the ground. Dragon bones? Strange copper books green with age? He pondered a moment, scratched at his beard, and lost his seat in the saddle just a fraction as his horse fretted. He leaned down mere inches to right himself as his horse stamped impatiently, but it was just enough.

Just enough that a bullet meant for the back of his head missed, whistling perilously close and taking his hat off.

Porter instinctively dropped to the ground as he heard voices call out behind in glee. "We got him!"

One of the digging Indians was hit in the chest as he rose. He dropped back to the earth in a wide embrace.

Bloody Creek Mary gave hell to her horse and plunged through the wall of trees and beyond, while the remaining dozen or so Indians who had been burying god knows what, scattered like ducks taking wing in every direction to the cover behind.

"I got him," said a deeper bass tinged growl with a slurring of speech.

"Stoney got him!"

Another shot brought a yelp from Dawg and the animal tore off into cover of the trees. That was bad, the animal was mute and never barked or yelped.

"You got the dog, too!"

At least now Porter knew who was shooting at him. That explained the slurred speech, he was missing a few teeth and probably still had swollen lips and face.

"Where'd that scar-faced squaw get to?"

"She lit out," answered either Pickax Pete or the rat-faced Thorne.

Porter laid face down in the soft earth. At least that had broken his fall and he didn't feel any sorer for it. He kept his head low and still, straining to see where his foes were.

Movement snaking through the trees like ghosts caught his eye. Luckily, there was still a good distance between them, almost fifty yards, especially considering he was the one in the center of a clearing and they had the cover of thick trees.

The soft earth had a gentle slope to his right where he could have a little bit of cover in the half ditch the Indians had been filling in. He had a firm grip on his dragoon, and he waited until he espied a clean shot to the foremost man. He hoped it was Stoney. If he shot the leader, the rest of them might break and run down the mountainside.

But they moved chaotically through the pines, aspens, and alder. It was hard to tell, as he lay still, who was who, and when his peripheral vison revealed a man outlined clean and free of the trees, Porter lifted the muzzle and fired.

The crack of the bullet and the slap of lead striking the man dead center, followed by an anguished gurgle, told Porter he hit the man square. He didn't wait to see who it was, he rolled quick to the slight depression for cover.

"He killed Nelson!"

A volley of shots came his way, blasting heaps of fresh reddish earth over him in a dust shower.

The ambushers paused to reload, but Porter guessed several must still be keeping a steely barrel trained at him. So much for making them panic when he killed one.

A few more wild shots flew his way, clawing at the ground all around him. It was too close for comfort. He pressed himself deeper into the earth and brushed away a soft spot to get his face lower. He touched something firm, it wasn't a rock, it was bone.

He yanked and withdrew a long white femur not unlike the dragon bone Fei Buk had shown him for a moment the night before. He was sure it wasn't the same one, this one was larger. He tossed it just in front of himself and a bullet promptly snapped it in half.

Porter returned fire as best he could, and he heard a yelp. Whether it was pain or fear he wasn't sure yet.

The man continued caterwauling. "I can't see."

"He missed you, ya damn fool!" came the comforting reply.

"No, I got splinters in my eyes from the tree. I'm blind."

Porter chuckled, that was almost as good as shooting the man dead. He guessed it was rat-faced Thorne. Who was left? Stoney, who might be swollen and not as good a shot as he could be. Pickax Pete? There was enough shooters that there had to be at least one more. Who?

A twig snapped and he glanced far to his rear and saw another man standing at the tree line. He had a direct bead on Porter with a raised pistol.

Bloody Creek Mary launched from the trees like a she-lion. Her bowie knife arced high and came down in a savage slash that tore the gunman open from shoulder to sternum and the heart beyond. Blood splashed in a geyser while a look of primal fear whitened the would-be killer's face. He still managed to pull the trigger, but his shot went wide, yards away from his intended target.

Porter took the opportunity to raise up a little and shoot at the men in front of him.

Mary took the dead man's gun and shot toward the ambushers, granting Porter enough time to move to a better position. From where they were, they could each shoot both down and across at the Mountain Hounds. It was a bad position for Stoney and the Mountain Hounds, and the bushwhackers knew it.

A wild cry from one of Slow Badger's people signaled new antagonists were in the fray.

An arrow stuck into a tree one of the bushwhackers was hiding behind. A cry of alarm from the man had him move a pace and Porter almost got him.

More war cries sounded, and Porter never felt so surrounded as he did in that moment. He wondered if he wouldn't get an arrow in his back while he was spread out wide facing the Mountain Hounds.

Porter glanced at Bloody Creek Mary, and she made the sign for all clear. He signaled back at the sound of the Indians coming closer and she repeated the all clear sign as if to say it was not a threat. That was one thing of many off his mind, if she was right. Just before this it had seemed to be falling apart.

"Stoney! I think the injuns are coming up behind us," said one of the men with more than a little alarm in his wavering voice.

Porter recognized Stoney's slurred speech when the big man said, "Take Thorne and get him on his horse. We're moving back. We'll get them later. Brown's gotta come down sometime."

Thorne still wailed in pain as another man led him behind thick enough trees that Porter couldn't get a worthwhile bead on any of them. He sent a few shots their way just to get them moving.

"Do you see Dawg?" Porter asked Mary.

"Slow Badger has him. They are caring for his wound."

"How bad is it?"

"Bad."

Porter cursed and took a chance to move closer.

A shot rang out, sending earth flying not a hand's breadth from him.

Porter ducked back to the slope for better cover.

Mary sent a few wild shots toward the enemy, but she signaled Porter that she couldn't see their foe, and she wasn't a good shot anyhow, having almost no experience with a gun.

But Stoney didn't know that. "We'll be back and tear your guts out, Brown! If the injuns don't do it first! Ha!"

He grunted as he climbed into his saddle, then he slapped his horse's hindquarters with his reins, and the familiar retreat of thundering hooves sounded as they charged back down the mountain.

Porter and Mary cautiously approached the gap where one of the Mountain Hounds lay dead.

"Looks like we only got two of them," said Porter, as he picked up the dead man's scattergun. It was a fine double-barreled piece, and still loaded.

"You blinded a third," she offered.

"Yep, but I didn't even recognize the one you got." Porter pointed out toward the trees where he could hear people moving and asked, "You sure things are all right with Slow Badger and the rest? What were they doing here?"

"Big medicine here."

He shook his head. "That still ain't much of an answer."

She shrugged. "Understand what you can."

"No telling how many more of them Mountain Hounds there are, and if they can't get to me, they are sure as shooting gonna cause trouble for Jack. I better hurry after them."

"Jack can handle himself."

"I can hope so, but I can't let anything happen. Can you take care of Dawg? I better get going after them." He charged into the brush and saw his horse not fifty paces away.

"They might be waiting at the bottom to ambush you."

Porter pushed through a thicket to reach his appaloosa. "Gotta take that chance and help even the odds for Jack. I can't let those Mountain Hounds all ride down like a storm on top of him with a damn tent for cover with just a shotgun and revolver."

"There is more to this," said Mary. "Slow Badger said…"

"They're your people, see if you can get it sorted for now," said Porter, as he leapt into the saddle.

"There are worse things waiting," she called.

"Don't let them eat my dog."

Bloody Creek Mary shook her head. "Fei Buk was correct about the Old Ones."

Porter shrugged. "I can't be worrying about that now while my friends and business are in danger."

"But the stars…"

"I'll come back for you, but I've gotta go help Jack before they jump him and burn the Round Tent," he called over his shoulder as he raced down the trail.

"The stars are right tonight!" she cried.

Porter had no time for that nonsense. He had a place to be, at the head of a wall of justice. Overhead the sun was obscured by lead-colored clouds, and the day seemed to fill with gloom.

DEATH DEALER

Sharp gusts of wind nipped at his neck and Porter was aware of soreness from last night's fight as he guided his horse down the rocky trail. Pitiless clouds above coalesced into the shape of looming thunderheads threatening heavy rain in the distance. Porter gingerly had his horse hurry down the slope. He was cautious of every bend in the trail and thick stand of trees. Anywhere he guessed an ambush could happen he eyed carefully before proceeding. He wished Dawg were there to hurry ahead and help smoke them out, but it couldn't be helped. He just hoped the mangy hound would be all right, but if he didn't hurry, maybe none of his friends here would be all right. Jack was a good man, and capable one on one, but not against a half-dozen of the Mountain Hounds and Stoney.

Sure, Zeke and Boles were likely there, but could they be counted on when things got rough? Unlikely, and Porter wouldn't leave Jack hanging like that. He cursed himself, he should have known Stoney and his pack would be out for blood. Well, he would set things right next time he saw the bushwhackers.

He was almost to the bottom where Williamson's camp was. The roar of the river was louder here, and he still hadn't seen any sign of the Mountain Hounds. Maybe they had hurried away to lick their wounds and take on an easier target. Maybe if they took the fight to Round Tent right away he could get them in the back while they focused on Jack and the others.

Glancing down at the hoof prints coming down the mountain, Porter's tracking skills allowed him to number six retreating horses; but to Porter's trained eye he could tell that only four of them carried men, the other two were being led.

He paused a moment at the last bend in the trail right before he reached bottom. He strained to listen to the woods but could discern nothing but the river and its continual droning song. He watched his horse's ears. The black appaloosa twitched but seemed content as if it had nothing more on its mind than carrying him back home.

The wind shifted and the friendly scent of a campfire came to him, promising warmth and food. He caught a hint of coffee, too.

Easing his appaloosa along the bend, he saw his antagonists. He had caught them unawares. They were encamped at Williamson's. Someone had even dragged his stiff body from the canvas tent and tossed it unceremoniously to the side of his rockerbox. The horses were gathered close by the river. The men were oblivious to his presence. Two by the fire and two more nearer the horses.

Porter drew his six-gun in one hand while resting the scattergun on the saddle horn. He held both his reins and the trigger for the shotgun at the ready. He blocked the trail, looking down on them. He eased the appaloosa a few steps toward his foes.

One man knelt on his haunches before the fire, getting ready to pull the coffee pot off the flames. He caught sight of Porter and let the pot drop back into the coals. He slowly stood, keeping his hands away from his gun belt. Thorne, who was blinded with a bandage over his eyes, sat beside the fire unaware. Some of the coffee splashed from the kettle and hit his leg, he cursed softly. "Dagnabit. What was that?"

"Stoney," said the one at the fire who had first seen Porter. Not eliciting a response fast enough, he repeated urgently, "Stoney!"

Pickax Pete and Stoney both had their backs to Porter. Pete was brushing down his horse while Stoney was taking a leak.

"What?" barked Stoney, as he gave himself a shake.

"You all are a piss poor bunch of bushwhackers," drawled Porter. "Throw down your guns or your lives."

Stoney spun about. His eyes darted to where each of his men were and where their guns were.

Porter had three barrels trained on them. His pistol was on Stoney while the double-barreled scattergun was on the two men beside the fire. A snarl washed over Pickax Pete's face, but he was also the farthest away, being beside the horses. He wasn't wearing a gun either—that still hung on his saddle horn.

"Who's there?" asked Thorne, turning his head back and forth despite his inability to discern anything.

The kettle with the coffee started to whistle.

Eyes flashed to guns and back to the eyes across from them.

Hands moved ever so slowly toward guns.

The whistle increased in steam power.

Eyes locked in death's embrace.

"Is someone gonna pull that off afore it burns?" asked a bullet-headed bald man who stepped out from Williamson's tent. He saw Porter had the drop on his friends and he reacted, trying to draw his own gun.

Porter blasted with the shotgun and moved his own pistol to shoot the man who was drawing down on him.

The shotgun blast took the man beside the fire and he fell back, a red mist lingering a moment over his corpse.

Porter hit the bald man in the chest, but his antagonist fired as he fell, hitting the appaloosa in the neck.

The horse screamed and shot upward, launching Porter from the saddle to the hard-packed ground.

Stoney drew his gun and fired but, in the turmoil, missed his mark. The crazed, wounded horse bounded between him and Porter and spooked the rest of the horses so they panicked and pulled at their own tethers in every direction, causing Pickax Pete to dodge away and lose his chance at retrieving his gun belt.

Slammed to the ground, Porter rolled just as the bald man fired again, missing by a mile.

Porter hit the bald man with the second blast of the shotgun, and the bullet-headed foe fell back against the tent, splashing it with crimson.

"Where is everybody?" shouted Thorne, standing. His outstretched hands groped for help amid the chaos.

Stoney, knocked back by the horse crazed fury, shot toward Porter again but missed. He ran to the opposite slope to flank Porter between himself and the flume. He shot again and again.

Porter was forced to move, rolling away. He shot but missed Stoney twice.

"Where is everybody? Help me!" cried Thorne.

"Shut up!" shouted Stoney.

Porter charged ahead, using Thorne as cover. Porter grasped Thorne's suspenders and held him like a shield as he moved to get around the flume for cover.

Thorne said, "Thanks for moving me friend."

Stoney didn't hesitate in shooting at them both and a bullet nicked Thorne in the shoulder.

Thorne cried out but struggled limply while Porter pushed them forward. He stumbled along, thinking a friend was moving him toward cover. He shouted, "Brown shot me in the shoulder. Kill him Stoney!"

Stoney shot again, this time striking Thorne in the stomach. Thorne cried out, "You kilt me, I'm dead."

Thorne went limp but Porter held onto the man's suspenders until he could get around the other side of the two-foot high flume for cover. He let Thorne fall into the rushing water and the body was dragged down the channel swiftly.

Stoney put a few holes in the flume, which sprung jets of water, but he could no longer see where Porter was hiding.

Porter crawled along the flume, readying himself to shoot, when he heard a hard thud behind him.

Turning back, he saw that Pickax Pete had just landed behind him, armed with his namesake.

Pickax had the tool raised high and it was coming down.

Porter could shoot him and be nailed to the ground, or he could move. He moved.

The pickax stabbed into the soft earth, catching just a hint of Porter's coat with it and pinning it to the ground.

Before he could pull the tool free, Pete was kicking at Porter. "You killed my friends, you son of a bitch!"

Porter lined his barrel up with Pete's head.

Pete's eyes widened with fear.

Click. He was empty.

"Ha! I got you-you sum bitch!" shouted Pete, as he kicked at Porter.

Out of ammo and Pete had yanked the pickax up again.

Porter lunged to get inside the arc of Pete's swing.

The Pickax came down and the handle bruised Porter's shoulder something fierce, but that was a helluva lot better than being skewered.

"Kill him!" cried Stoney, as a shot rang out and ricocheted from the boulders just behind Porter.

"You trying to kill me, too?" shouted Pickax Pete. The miss was too close for comfort since he and Porter were caught in a killer's embrace.

Porter hit with a left hook and sent Pete sprawling to the ground.

Stoney shot again and this time the bullet ripped through the elbow on Porter's coat. The lead ball yanked at the thick leather, threatening take it on a faraway journey, but it missed Porter's flesh.

Dropping to the ground and the cover of the flume, Porter grabbed for another cylinder for his dragoon. He fumbled in his pocket for the cylinder while Pickax Pete crawled away from him.

"Where you at Pete? Kill him!" snarled Stoney.

"I don't want you to shoot me in the trying," responded Pete.

Porter found the cylinder.

"You yeller polecat!" shouted Stoney, as he shot the flume twice. His wheel gun clicked on empty.

Pickax Pete jumped up, the hickory haft of his pickax in hand again. He glanced at Porter fiddling with his dragoon, while Stoney was busy reloading too.

Porter loaded the cylinder.

Pete raised the pickax over his head for a devastating blow.

Porter flicked his wrist, bringing the gun to bear, and shot Pete between the eyes.

The pickax fell but only from gravity not a deathblow. Pete's eyes crossed and he fell backward.

Porter took a deep breath. The pickax and bullets had sheared several holes through his coat. Awful close.

He glanced over the edge of the flume, looking for Stoney.

A shot rang out, tearing the lip off the flume just a pace away from himself.

Porter gritted his teeth and moved down the line a few feet. He tried to gauge Stoney's whereabouts anyway he could. He strained to see the reactions of the nearby horses, but they had panicked and were all out of sight.

The dull roar of the river masked any hint of sound.

Stoney had been coming closer. He must be just on the other side of the flume.

Porter glanced at the bottom to see if there was any space he could see beneath the thing to better get at the big man, but the flume sat firm against the ground, heavy with the ever-running water.

Launching up, Porter sent several shots right over the top at where he though Stoney hid. But there was no one there.

Where had he gone?

A WILD MAN

The ruckus of someone stumbling through the brush a short distance away gave the answer. Stoney had retreated from what looked like a suicidal position.

Porter shot once more in his general direction, then reloaded.

Glancing toward his appaloosa, he saw the animal was down and not likely to get up again. He strode to it and whispered, "Damnit." He pulled the trigger and ended the horse's suffering.

The gang's horses lingered a short distance away but moving toward them would expose himself to a severe lack of cover, while Stoney was still making a terrible sound crashing through the trees. Too risky to get a horse just yet, so he waited beside the flume a moment longer.

What was his angle, Porter wondered? He was making too much sound to be sneaking into a better position to snipe at him, besides, he didn't have a rifle.

A few wild shots from the pistol went off, but near as Porter could tell none of them were even close to heading his way. Was Stoney shooting at him as a distraction for something else? Did he have another man out there looking to flank Porter while he did a stupid bluff? Unlikely, the man in the tent had been a surprise and it was Porter's own fault for not counting the seven horses as he reached the bottom. They had left a man at the bottom as a lookout just in case of any other troubles. But there wouldn't be anyone else out here.

There was another wild shot and a loud snorting amidst a snapping of twigs and underbrush.

Stoney cried out in fear.

Were Slow Bear and the other Indians pursuing him? That didn't seem right. Besides, the snorts were too loud for a man.

Stoney darted out of the woods, but not toward Porter in an attack, he headed as fast as he could straight to the river in a crazed panic. "Run!" he cried, glancing only just once sidelong at Porter. He no longer held a gun. He must have dropped it with his last shot spent. He inexplicably continued his course to the river in a mad dash and threw himself into the cold water, heading out for where the current would carry him off.

Was this some kind of insane trick?

The great tearing through the trees continued to get closer. Porter wondered if there was a grizzly about to launch free of the woods. But would even a grizzly have given a man like Stoney such primal terror? He glanced about the camp, hoping for something with a bigger bore than his dragoon.

Porter stood his ground in wonderment.

Stoney was in three feet deep of water and beginning to be tugged away by the current.

The crashing through the underbrush drew closer and a wild black shape materialized in the center of it all. It was incredibly tall, perhaps eight feet, and Porter wondered if it was a gigantic bull moose.

But a huge, hair covered man-thing stepped out and looked at Porter. Its red eyes blazing with hate.

Porter stood slack-jawed, staring at the incredible monster. "I'll be dipped," he said to himself, realizing he had left his mouth open a good while too long.

It stared back, breathing deep. It snorted once then let out the most terrible roar Porter had ever heard in his life. Porter felt the beast's call vibrating deep into his chest. It seemed like the earth itself shook from the terrific sound.

In that moment, Porter no longer heard the dull perpetual sound of the river.

The wild man stared at him again, breathing deep with lungs that sounded like a blacksmith's bellows.

Lost at what to do, Porter did the first primal thing that came to mind. He didn't shoot, he had forgotten about his gun, but he didn't cower in fear either. He shouted back at the wild man as loud and angry as he could. "Argh!"

By comparison it was a pup howling at a lion, but this lion heard him.

The gigantic wild man picked up a boulder as big around as a wagon wheel. Porter gaped in awe at the immense strength to even budge the stone, let alone pick it up.

The wild man threw the boulder, not at Porter, but perilously close. It made a titanic splash in the river. The hairy man raised his arms, beat his chest, and gibbered as if in triumph.

A cry of fear from Stoney farther out in the river brought Porter back to the wider world. He had been lost in the moment. With great difficulty, Porter tore his gaze from the giant wild man to glance at Stoney out in the river.

Stoney was splashing out into the waters and drifting away toward Murderer's Bar.

The wild man's breathing was thunderous, like the chugging of a steamboat's paddle. He grunted at Porter then roared again. The sound echoed from the far-off mountain tops.

Porter was aware of no other sound in the world.

Porter glanced at the still swelling spot where the boulder had crashed. The river swirled dark and muddy. He returned a steely gaze to the wild man.

The wild man took a step forward and grinned.

Porter didn't take it as a friendly grin. It looked more like a show of force like, *these are what I'm going to use to eat you.*

His blood turned to ice water, his legs ready to buckle, but Porter would never just take the easy walk into the dark without a fight. He whispered a prayer, guessing this would be his final moment. At least he would see lost friends soon.

The giant charged.

Porter brought his pistol up and shot the brute three times in his left breast. Tufts of hair and dust burst from the behemoth's chest, but Porter saw no blood.

He was out of shots. He fumbled in his coat for another cylinder. Something metallic touched his hand he though perhaps it was another cap and bull come loose. He withdrew the strange golden pin.

A solitary ray of sunlight caught on the pin and dazzled the eye.

The wild man snorted angrily, spun around, took a massive step to the left, and faded back into the trees. This time there was no crash of thunder as it moved away. It silently vanished like a black cat into starless shadow.

Porter watched a long time thinking it was going to charge him and smash him underfoot, but it was gone. Was it a bluff? There was no blood. He had hoped to take out the thing's heart, but it didn't appear wounded.

The sound of the river and birds returned shortly.

Porter wondered at that. Had it been just the unreal experience of seeing the hairy wild man, or was there something else? Strange coincidence that he had pulled the pin out and the wild man ceased his charge and retreated into the woods. Was it related? Hadn't Mary said something about it being a pin of protection?

Porter sunk down beside the flume and breathed deep. He dug in his torn coat and reloaded another cylinder into his dragoon. He found the scattergun and loaded that, too. Only then, when he felt ready for anything, did he reach into his inner pouch and find a flask. He took a long pull of whiskey and watched the thick dark woods.

Nothing. No sound of anything having been there at all. Porter kept a wary eye but took another long pull of refreshing liquid courage. He stepped forward and glanced along the ground, trying to see any sign of the hairy man. There were no tracks he could see along the hard-stony ground.

A branch overhead showed that if anything, once he stood beneath it, the wild man might have been even taller than he first thought. The sheer size had been incredible.

Had he been poisoned? Hit in the head and imagined the whole thing? No, Stoney saw it first, panicked, shot at it, and even ran into the river risking drowning to escape it. They had not shared a delusion, he decided. That had really happened.

He rubbed his hands across his face and splashed some water on it.

What had Fei Buk said last night? The stars were right for old ones here? Could that giant wild man be an old one?

He sat down. Realized he was still sitting in a scene of grisly death, but the slain bushwhackers seemed inconsequential compared to what he had just been through. Porter liked to think of himself as a man prepared for anything, but this had flummoxed him. He saw a cigar resting on the ground near the still crackling fire. He picked it up, lit it on the coals, and puffed mightily.

Porter knew he should have been grabbing one of the available horses, but he had to take in the moment and deal with it first. It seemed unbelievable. He finally stood up to go and fetch a horse when he heard something whispering on the wind from the nearby woods. It sounded soft and feminine. Was it Bloody Creek Mary calling him?

"Porter," it called from somewhere farther into the woods. "Porter."

It sure sounded like Mary.

"Mary? Is that you?"

"Porter," the voice summoned again.

He went toward it. It didn't sound troubled. She didn't sound wounded or hurt, but it was urgent and pleading.

Porter found himself stumbling off the beaten track and heading into the dark forest.

"Porter," it beckoned, "over here."

He tripped on a log he didn't realize was lying in his path, he was so focused on reaching the source.

"Over here."

He thought he saw her outline near a tree, the light was refracting strangely, but the willowy shadow resembled the lithe Indian woman.

"Over here, Porter."

"Where are you going?" asked a new voice, breaking his dreamlike concentration.

He resisted turning around to look. A powerful feeling that he should press on into the woods persisted.

"Over here."

"What are you doing?" challenged the new voice. It sounded harsh and unpleasant.

Porter wheeled about to face whoever had disturbed him. It was Mary standing twenty paces behind him on the trail. He wheeled to glance toward where he thought she had been calling him, perhaps another fifty yards into the forest. The shadowy outline was gone. Only a red, moss-covered tree trunk remained.

"Is someone in there?" Mary asked.

Porter trudged back to her and the trail. "I thought it was you. Could have sworn I heard you calling my name."

She shook her head. "You know I was up the mountain at the dig. I heard shots and came down on foot."

He peered accusingly back at the woods. "I heard something."

"Where is your gun?" She watched and waited for him to speak.

Porter reached to his gun belt and was dumbfounded to find it empty. He took a gander at the log he had hopped over to see if he had dropped the dragoon, but it was not there either. He passed Mary and the trail and looked at the incredible scene of carnage. His dragoon and shotgun were resting beside the fire. Right where he had been when he first heard the call of the voice in the forest. What on earth could have made him forget and leave his weapons lying there?

"What happened?" she asked.

Porter motioned at the dead men all over Williamson's camp. "I got the drop on 'em. Got everyone except Stoney."

"Where is he?"

"He... uh?" Porter scratched at his neck. "I forgot."

Mary ran her hands over his scalp and neck. "Did you get hit?"

"No. Got thrown. They shot Bess, I had to put her down."

Mary took in the scene. "But Stoney is gone? Were you chasing him into the woods?"

"No, he... uh. Where did he go?" Porter pondered. He realized he couldn't remember anything except the gun fight. He retraced his steps about the camp and puzzled. "I shot those two. Used Thorne as a shield. Stoney killed him. Then I shot Pete. I went to shoot Stoney, but he ran into the woods, then he came out..."

Mary followed Porter's tale of carnage knowing full well there was more to it than his simple retelling. She followed a track line to the edge of the woods then saw tracks rushing toward the river.

"Did he go to the river? Was there a canoe?"

"No, he... uh, jumped in and swam downriver."

She cocked her head at him. "Why? Did you have the drop on him?"

"Not exactly no I... uh." He couldn't remember quite right. What had happened? He remembered all of that, but there seemed to be a blank spot in his mind's eye.

"Then you were moving into the woods, but you said Stoney went to the river," said Mary, trying to elicit a response.

"Yeah, I heard something in the woods. I thought it was you."

She shook her head. "That was not me. I would not do that. I would come to you." She peered sharply at the forest. "It called to you?"

"Yeah," said Porter, sitting on a log and rubbing at his temples.

"It might have been one of the Furry People."

"Furry People?"

Mary nodded. "It is not good to follow their call. Those that follow, do not come back."

"Sounds like a will o' the wisp."

"I do not know those words, but is bad?"

Porter nodded. He knew he was forgetting something, but couldn't recollect what exactly. "Hey, where's Dawg?"

Mary pointed back up the trail. "Slow Badger has him. They are bandaging him up."

"You sure?"

"Yes."

"Well, since only Stoney is left of the Mountain Hounds, and they shot my horse, let's lay claim on these others and go get Dawg and head back home. If Stoney doesn't drown, he'll be trying to warm up all night long. It will be getting dark soon enough."

Mary pursed her lips and nodded and helped Porter gather the horses.

They rode back up the mountainside, until they reached the spot where they had met the digging Indians the first time.

GHOST HORN SPEAKS

They turned to head into the trees, but Slow Badger was already there, carrying Dawg out.

Dawg looked happy to see Porter and Mary, his tongue was hanging out and he was mutely panting his hellos.

Slow Badger said something to Mary and put Dawg down. He limped toward Porter and licked his hand.

Porter kneeled. "Sorry, Dawg." He let his pet lick his cheek.

Mary explained, "Slow Badger says it was clean and went through his upper leg and tail, but it is gone."

Porter looked over Dawg and realized the missing appendage. His brow raised. "They shot off my dog's tail?"

Slow Badger produced the tail and said something Porter couldn't understand, but it sounded like an apology.

"He says he knows those men are killers of his people, and he is grateful you fought them."

Porter stood and glanced back at the two dead men. "Nothing to thank me for, those bastards were here to try and cut my cord."

Mary said, "They don't know that, but he also said they are sorry for what they did to take back the key and bones. But they didn't kill anyone."

Porter grimaced, wondering if he had another fight on his hands. "Key and bones? Aren't they admitting to killing MacDonald? You said you thought they were all in on it."

Slow Badger spoke a long harsh sentence that Mary translated.

"I was wrong. He said they took the bones but nothing else. They want the key, the book, returned."

Mary translated and Slow Badger answered begrudgingly but pointed at the corpse of the dead tribal member.

"He says that he and Prairie Dog were the ones who went to steal back the book and that Prairie Dog lost the pin of protection. He did not want them to hurt anyone and start a war with white men. Someone else got the book before them."

Slow Badger made a sign with his hands, but Porter didn't follow what that meant either.

"What about all them bones I saw them burying here?"

"The ones from across the sea, the Chinese had stolen the bones from the burial grounds. They had to be returned. But the Chinese were slain by someone in the dark. He says the killers left the bones, so they took them back and left the bodies there because they did not want to be blamed for the murder."

Porter chewed at the edges of his beard. "What about the book?"

"That was taken by the killer. He says it was dark in the tent and they got inside first while MacDonald was still sleeping, but a white man came in and took the book and killed MacDonald."

"A white man? Who? Why didn't they jump him outside the tent?"

Slow Badger made faces and gestures, but it was clear he was trying to emulate Stoney and company.

"He had many men with him, with many guns. Too many, so they waited and escaped just before we got there."

Porter corrected, "Before I got there. Did you see them?"

She shook her head.

Porter spit. "Alright, so it was Stoney. How would that polecat know about the book?"

Slow Badger spoke and Mary translated once again. "It was Thorne."

Porter swore and rubbed at his face. "And the pin?"

"He says MacDonald was bleeding out and they went to help him, when he grabbed them not realizing who had slain him and who they were. It was a struggle to escape the dying old man. Prairie Dog lost the pin to the dying man's grasp."

Porter held a hand up. "Wait. If the Chinese found the book and it was hidden under that cairn for who knows how long, why did Slow Badger suddenly come to get it back? How did they even know it was there?"

Slow Badger spoke quickly, and Porter couldn't follow a word, but Mary continued her translation.

"He say the book is key to the door. Bones are of the old guardians from long ago. They knew the key was buried on the mountain, but they would not look for it. But now that it is found, it must be returned and reburied in secret."

Porter shook his head. "What door? What guardians?"

Mary continued, "Ghost Horn will speak, since you have slain the murderers and even dealt with the Furry People."

"Furry people?" Porter asked and then the strange memory of the wild hairy man came flooding back and he was almost overwhelmed reliving the experience. He closed his eyes and shivered at the harrowing event. How had he forgotten it and had it come flooding back like that? There was some supernatural power at play here.

Mary took hold of his shoulder and shook him. "It is like that when you meet them, but worse things are waiting beyond the door."

"How would you know?" gasped Porter.

"Ghost Horn told me."

"Ghost Horn?"

"He is here," she said, pointing back to the tree line.

A tall old man with long white braids running down each side of his face stepped into the clearing. He was wrapped in a red blanket and had a deer's antler woven into his hair. Porter recognized him as the shaman, Ghost Horn.

Mary continued, "He say he will show you what this sacred place is. He knows what you have done. By your actions today, you are a worthy guardian, too."

It was getting dark and while the wind had died down, the chill in the air was sharp.

Ghost Horn beckoned for Porter to follow and then without watching, he turned around and strode back into the tree line. Several braves including Slow Badger were nearby and they too motioned for Porter and Mary to come. Even Dawg, who had been very pleased to be reunited with Porter, loped after them.

"Guess we better get along and see what the man has to say then, huh?" asked Porter, looking to Mary.

"Yes, you should," she said, before she too followed after.

Porter gritted his teeth and strode on, the last in line. He couldn't help but look over his shoulder, wondering if anything was watching. The casual mention of the "Furry

People" had been unsettling to say the least. It was as if these people just accepted that there were monsters in their world, and it was no cause for alarm. Same as a bear or mountain lion, just one of those things out there striding through the forest.

Not terribly far down a thin game trail was a level slope where a handful of tepees were cloistered together. Ghost Horn went into one and Slow Badger held the flap open and gestured for Porter and Mary to follow. Dawg needed no invitation and went right in, curling up toward the back.

Once Porter and Mary sat across the fire from Ghost Horn, he passed a pipe to them and they each took turns about the small coiling fire that only just barely lit up the room. After everyone had several turns, Ghost Horn spoke.

"My tongue is not always good with your words, so I may sometimes use ones that I know, that you do not know and my tribal daughter from another father will help me speak them," he said, gesturing to Mary.

"I think I understand you," said Porter.

"This is good," replied Ghost Horn. "Many moons ago, before your people came to these lands and before my people came to these lands, others were here. They dwelt in the fields and valleys, they lived in the mountains and in the earth too. They rode giant beasts that exist no more and even went speeding across the face of the great waters. Sometimes I think when an earthquake shakes the land that they are waking up, for while it may seem that they are gone, they are still here in hiding, and they are asleep. Many times I have wondered if some of them are good, but most of the stories that my grandfathers taught me was that they were evil and used their great skills and technologies much like the whites do now, and they made war and they robbed one another and did murder many for gain. Some may have resisted and not done these terrible things, but they are removed from the land and are no more. My grandfathers knew that the cataclysms that came from the sky, like falling mountains that burned, came and destroyed these Old Ones' civilizations. Those that could, went and hid themselves up in the earth while all of their cities and kingdoms in the fields and valleys and mountains were destroyed. But those that still dwell in the earth, knew that to survive they must sleep away the eons and be as dreamers. Many things are still hidden up in the earth, weapons of war, books of knowledge that would make all the white man's technology seem like a child's. But many of these things are not ready for the world of now and must remain hidden. I know you have seen some of these things, that you have touched them and know I speak the truth. I know you have seen the Furry People and you saw the bones of long dead gods and guardians. I say to you, let sleeping gods lie. Let them sleep."

Porter chewed at his beard and wondered if Ghost Horn would say anything more, but he didn't, he just sat opposite Porter and stared at him with obsidian eyes.

"Alight. I won't wake them," he said at last.

"That is good," said Ghost Horn abruptly.

"Well," Porter asked, "can you tell me what or who the Furry People are?"

"They were made by the Old Ones like a child might make a toy man out of sticks and clay. My grandfather said that the Old Ones took a piece of a star flesh and with the flesh of men the Old Ones merged them. They are like us, but not like us. One of the Furry People might have the strength of many braves and they can walk unseen if they wish, passing through the shadow lands, but they also cannot commune with the creator, the Great Spirit. They are cut off from his presence, and when they die, they cannot go to the Happy Hunting Grounds. Sometimes I wonder if the white man

117

cannot commune with the Great Spirit either, but my daughter from another father says you are a good man with Big Medicine and that the Great Spirit has smiled upon you."

"I don't want to go treading into the earth and waking any sleeping gods," said Porter. "I never would have believed in things like the Furry People or the sleeping old ones. I don't wish to disturb them."

"But you had the key to the door. You bought it for money. That is not good," said Ghost Horn in a direct fashion. Porter couldn't help but feel like, coming from the old man, it was a heated dressing down.

"I only knew that it was an old book and I wanted to keep it safe. It was not my intent to use it to awaken any old ones. I wanted to show it to wise men."

"It is not for those kinds of worldly-wise men in the cities. It was crafted by the Old Ones as a key to one of the doors to their hidden place to dream. They should not be awakened."

"I understand that. I was not going to do that." He looked to Mary and said, "Explain to him I thought it was only a book and not a key to any door."

Mary spoke quickly in the native tongue and seemed to confirm Porter's words.

Ghost Horn listened and nodded, then asked, "But where is the key now?"

"I don't know. I had it and then someone came into my saloon and murdered a man and stole it. They stole back those dragon bones from the Chinese who dug them up here too. All that I have left is this pin." He produced the pin and showed it to Ghost Horn.

"You may keep that. It is a protection from the Old Ones," said Ghost Horn. "My daughter said you were born to be a guardian of sacred things."

Porter glanced at Mary. "Not me. You all can have it back."

Ghost Horn shook his head. "It is yours for now. Some troubles will come soon until the key is found and put back. The sleeping gods must stay asleep. But the stars are right for trouble with the key lost, and then you will need that strength of protection."

"Well, I got enough of my own," said Porter, patting his dragoon. He tossed the pin back to Ghost Horn.

The old man frowned deeply.

Mary swore under her breath and took the pin and stuck it on Porter's jacket lapel. "You will keep it," she whispered urgently.

"Fine. But I still don't know where the book is. My only guess after everything today is that Stoney has it. But who knows where? I imagine he is gonna try and sell it, not awaken any Old Ones."

"You must get it back from him, so that my people can hide it up again," said Mary as urgently as she had ever spoken.

Porter looked at her and nodded. "I aim to make things square with that bushwhacker, might as well hand that thing off to you, too."

"That is good," said Ghost Horn.

Porter wondered after things Ghost Horn said once he realized it mirrored things Fei Buk had spoken of. "What does 'the stars are right' mean?"

Ghost Horn looked up to the conical roof of the tepee where the smoke rose and vented out to the dark sky and stars beyond. He pondered a long while, then said, "I think I can explain in a way you may understand. White men have forgotten the energies that come from the stars and planets. They affect us still and the powers from these bodies can be like the ocean tide. Sometimes it is strong and high, it protects us. Sometimes it is low and weak. When it is weak, those things held back might come forth like crabs on the beach. When the tide is low, bad things can be revealed and let loose to wander where we human beings are." He shuddered and, taking the pipe, blew smoke around the tepee and chanted for a long moment in a tongue Porter could not understand.

Mary whispered, "He does this to cleanse the bad energies from even discussing the Old Ones."

Porter looked at the old man and asked, "What if I can't find that book though? What then?"

Ghost Horn, suddenly animated, said, "The Old Ones will dream dreams and see the key is found by wicked men. If the door is opened, they will walk out and doom the land. Even if the door is not opened, they will send their dreams, their nightmares, out into the world and make them a reality. It must be found and returned. They must stay asleep."

"I'll see what I can do then," said Porter.

GOD LOVES FOOLS

Rather than ride back down the trail at night and possibly into another ambush, they stayed that night at the little collection of tepees. First light, Porter was up and he, Mary, and Dawg rode back to Murderer's Bar. It was a chilly morning with fog rolling in off the river creating an eerie atmosphere across the landscape. Some miners were up and at it already and you could hear gold pans being spun and pickaxes striking stone, but not see any of them.

Porter imagined it might sound like hell, if you threw in a dash of wailing souls.

A figure loomed into view as if the fog had parted for him like water from the keel of a ship. The man just stood there in the path, and Porter reached for his gun. The old man lifted his head and Porter remembered him as the grinning old miner with the penetrating gaze.

"Work still to be done," said the old man.

"Yup," answered Porter sullenly, leading his horse around the old man who had still not moved.

As Porter passed him, the old man faced him, looked up, and said, "The stars are gonna be right tonight. You best make things right."

Porter, puzzled, turned in the saddle to look at the old man again, but he was gone. The early morning fog swirled about the camp, but he doubted the old man could have vanished so suddenly.

"Did you see that old man?" he asked Mary, who was riding up behind him.

"I didn't see anyone," she said.

Porter frowned, wondering what the trick of the early morning light had played on his senses.

He cautiously rode up to the Round Tent saloon and was pleased to see it looking unscathed.

"Check it out, Dawg," he said.

Dawg went forward, stuck his nose in the tent flaps, and went inside. A moment later Jack exited.

"He woke me up. That was a long night. I expected you back a whole lot earlier," said Jack.

"Meant to be but had a couple run-ins with Stoney's bunch."

"Oh? How'd that go?"

"I got all of 'em except Stoney himself. Then we spoke with Ghost Horn to learn a bit more about the book and such as it is."

"That what happened to Dawg's tail?"

Porter grimaced, looking at his dog. "Yep, one of the bastards shot him in the shoulder and took his tail off with another round. I think we used up six of them."

Jack nodded. "I'd say Stoney might have at least that many more he counts on roundabouts. Maybe more."

"I reckon so, too. You got any help?"

Jack shook his head and grinned. "I sent Zeke and Boles off to the do the Sacramento run. I think they ought to get back today. Figured I'd spare you the job, things being what they are."

"Awful risky. What if they get jumped or worse?"

Jack shrugged. "God loves fools. I think they'll make it back."

"All right, well, Mary and I are here now, you go on and get some sleep, but keep your shooter handy."

"I will. Good night. I mean, good day." Jack walked toward his tent not far off in the trees on the hillside.

"I'll make some breakfast," said Mary. "But we need to go find that bushwhacker."

Porter grinned at her using his terminology. He had never heard her use that word before, course she had said as much in the last day as she had for the last month. "Sounds good. We'll find him soon enough. We'll let Jack rest and wait for the boys to get back before we go out again."

Mary frowned. "It must be found."

"And we will look, but we gotta be ready."

Half a day later Porter was still relaxing his aching muscles and nursing some whiskey between dirty looks from Mary, when Zeke and Boles came in. Their clothing was dirtier than usual, torn and ragged, and each of them had a dozen cuts, bruises, and oozing gashes all over their bodies. Zeke had a fat lip and Boles a black eye.

"What the hell happened to you two?" asked Porter.

Dawg leapt up and sniffed at the two of them and then slunk away as if disturbed at their very scent.

Porter got a whiff and wrinkled his nose in displeasure.

"What happened to Dawg's tail?" asked Boles.

"Never mind that. Tell me what happened to you two." demanded Porter.

Zeke answered, "We found out where Stoney is, and he is brewing up some trouble for you."

"That information might have been useful to me yesterday," said Porter.

Zeke and Boles looked at each other. Zeke spoke up, "We didn't have that information yesterday, boss."

"We only found out late last night, yes sir," added Boles.

"I'm sorry, go on."

"Well, Jack sent us off to do the Sacramento run since you weren't back and we didn't know when you'd be back. He seemed to think it was the most valuable thing we could do."

"Go on," said Porter, mulling it over.

"Well, we fetched the wagon and team and we got there alight. We went to the brewery and bought a wagon load."

"On credit, yes sir, Jack said we had to do it on credit," broke in Boles.

"Yeah, so we're coming on back, but Boles thought we ought to stop and get a drink and bite for ourselves before we did the long haul back, on account of we was each pushing the horses as hard as we could to get back lickety split."

"Are my horses alight?"

"Yes sir, yes sir, they is doing just fine, we fed and watered and rubbed 'em down, yes sir," said Boles.

"Get to the point," said Porter.

"We were stopped in at Coloma and went to the tavern. Had some grub and then came back out to find Stoney and a couple of his crew there looking over the team and such, they was planning on robbing the wagon. We said, 'hey now, what do you think you are a doing here' and they laughed at us and said it was an honest mistake," said Zeke.

"But I don't think it were, yes sir," broke in Boles.

Zeke continued, "So we told them to get out of there, that it was your property and they'd get some from you if they didn't call it quits."

"Then?" asked Porter, growing all the more impatient.

"Well, sir, they knocked us down and Stoney, he says he has it in for you and yours and that he was gonna take the property and we would have to like it."

"That's right, yes sir," repeated Boles. "They knocked us down and peed on us and said we had to take it cuz of you, sir. they said you was gonna be dead soon anyway and so we got out of there afore it got worse, yes sir."

Porter frowned at them.

Zeke piped up. "We got the wagon, team, and almost all the whiskey back for you though. They took the wagon only as far as Stoney's place and they all were carousing and drinking and smoking in there."

Porter raised his eyebrows in surprise. That the two near-do-wells even had the guts to follow the thieves and find out where they had taken the team was a pleasant surprise.

"We followed them to a big tent where the nine of 'em were drinking. Stoney himself was sitting on a big chair, smoking his cigar. He was holding some strange copper thing in his hands. It reminded me of a lady's fan, but I ain't never seen a fan like that before."

"Me neither, yes sir," added Boles. "Never seen anything like it."

The mention of the golden fan caught Porter's interest. "How big would you say it was? And how big around did the pieces look?"

Zeke scratched at his neck. "I guess about yea big." He held his hands out in a size eerily reminiscent of the size of the book when Porter had swung it open on its access point. Zeke continued, "And it looked like it was so big around it was almost a circle."

Porter nodded. Pieces were coming together. "Go on," he urged.

"Well we had a plan of sorts. We first went and got some gloves from Carlyle's, and then we got some poison oak and smeared it all over their saddles and reins and threw a clump of it among their gear on the outside of the tent. Didn't know if any of that would work, but figured it was worth a shot. Just to put some hurt on them after what they done, kicking mud in our eyes."

"And peeing on us, yes sir," added Boles.

"Yeah, that was most unpleasant," griped Zeke.

"Yes sir," broke in Boles, "then we wanted to make them mad and chase us, so we went and stood our front of their tent where they could see us at the edge of the firelight."

Porter asked, "Didn't you think they would shoot you?"

"Yes sir, there was a good chance of that, but we wanted to fool 'em into thinking they could just beat us again instead."

Porter raised his brows, utterly surprised at their bold inventiveness.

"So, we had pulled a rope real tight across the way at shin level, and then standing outside of that in the dark, we came up to their tent and started singing and carrying on ourselves."

"Yep, we sang about Stoney his self. We sang a song we made up on the spot, calling it about 'Stoner the Boner', and we did a dance and stuck our bare asses out at them."

Boles laughed. "Yes sir. And they made like they were going to charge us and I remember Cleve said that he would fornicate us to death, but then Stoney, he held 'em back a moment and let us continue doing our song a minute longer, it was downright uncomfortable it dragging on like that. We didn't expect him to let us finish. He was just a staring at us all cold-like. That was the part that started to scared me the most, but then he finally puffed on his cigar again and says, 'Get 'em!'"

Porter looked at the two of them, and after a spell of silence, he asked exasperatedly, "And?"

"We ran! We ran like hell, thinking they was gonna kill us. I tell you I never ran so hard in my life. They run out and tripped on the rope we waylaid them with and then some went to get the horses and got the poison oak all over their hands and arms. And funny thing is, we got mixed up and thought we were heading to the right place, we thought we would hide out at the Halfway House but then when we got there, we realized things only looked familiar, but we was backwards we weren't at the Halfway House at all, we went to the wrong building all the way across the range. It was even white-washed the same and had a well dug out front that matched, so we were fooled in our panic."

"Saved our backsides, I tell you what, because the way we meant to come well they thought they were heading us off up by the crossroads, but our mistake saved our skins. So, we back trailed away from them, then waited till almost morning and then took our sweet time being extra careful sneaking past the whole of Buckeye Flats to get here soon as we could."

"But you lost the pack and team?"

"Yes sir," said Boles. "But only for a few hours on account of they was gonna kill us."

"We double-backed an hour or two later when they was still out hunting all over for us in the dark. So, we got the pack and team and most all of the whiskey. They only unloaded and drank a couple cases."

"Cases?"

"Sorry boss, take it out of my pay."

Porter shook his head. "Naw, you got the team and wagon back and that's something. I shot half of his other boys yesterday and now it looks like I'm gonna have to clean house on what's left."

"What are we gonna do?"

"How many are there?" asked Porter.

Zeke and Boles counted between each other, naming off the gang as they knew them. "Well there's Stoney his self, Cleve his second, Donaldson, Harry Reed, Glasgow Red, Spicer, the Tartar, Arch, and one more, Leeds I think."

"It's Leeds," affirmed Boles. "He's got horrible teeth. Big snaggly things like a boar."

"So, nine total?" asked Porter.

"Yes, sir," said Boles.

Porter took the shotgun from the table and handed it to Boles. "We are gonna stay vigilant and put some lead into them soon as we see 'em."

Zeke looked over his shoulder worriedly. "But they might come here after dark."

Porter nodded. "I expect they will if we stay put and just let them come."

"But a tent ain't no place to be stopping lead."

"I didn't say we were gonna wait for them polecats. I only said we would put some lead into them. Now let's get ready to go find them. This war is gonna have to end fast before it gets too bloody for our side."

Boles nodded. "Well, that's a plan then ain't it? Yes, sir."

LEAD IS THE HUNGRIEST METAL

Porter made sure someone kept an eye open out front while the rest of them prepared for war. It would be a small enough war numerically, but deadly serious to everyone involved. Porter cursed himself that he had ignored the trouble with the Mountain Hounds gang this long. There hadn't been anyone else willing to put their life on the line against those desperadoes and he should have known it would come down to him. They had pushed their weight around at the mining camps long enough.

Porter loaded multiple cylinders and put them into several different pockets in his vest, jacket, and pants. He then took a spade and went and dug not twenty feet away out back. It wasn't deep, and Mary wondered at what he was doing.

"Are you digging a grave before you kill them?"

Porter chuckled. "Naw, a couple weeks before you came here to work I had buried this as a safety net."

"Money?"

"No, something better for the pickle we're in."

His spade struck something solid and he cleared away the earth on one side, then prying the shovel beneath it, he levered and brought the edge of the trunk up. He then grasped a leather handle on one side and pulled. It was stuck. He wedged the shovel in again and despite the grime, won the box free. He tore off a deerskin that had been placed over the whole of it and then unlatched it.

Inside, he had back up ammunition and arms. There was another pair of pistols, numerous knives, a tomahawk, several black powder tins, three Sharps rifles and a whole lotta lead. "I'm just glad that greasy deerskin kept everything dry. I was a little worried."

Bloody Creek Mary nodded in satisfaction at the buried armory. "Do I get one?"

"Sure, you do. But being as you don't have a lot of skill shooting yet, I suggest you keep the scattergun and plenty of shells. But I can sure teach you how to load and shoot one of these, too." He handed her one of the Sharps rifles.

Jack said, "I was wondering where you had those."

"I was saving them for a rainy day," said Porter.

"Looks like rain now," admitted Jack.

"The boys about ready?"

"Ready as they'll ever be, I reckon. They ain't never gone to a fight like this."

"Few folks have second chances. If they want to bail out, they're free to, but they ought to know their skins won't be worth spit if we fail."

Zeke and Boles came around the corner. "We're with you."

Bloody Creek Mary nodded, a smile almost showing on her stoic face as she handled the Sharps.

"Then let's take this score to their house instead of ours," said Porter. "Time to go Dawg."

Dawg leapt up, waggling his butt like he still had a tail.

Dusk wasn't far away, and they thundered down the road. It wouldn't be too far a ride for good horses between there and Coloma and Stoney's hideaway.

The road wound around the hills and through thick pines where sunlight dashed against them making tiger stripes on the forest floor.

They rounded a bend and came head on against a like-minded group of riders. Stoney's men, the Mountain Hounds.

When a hard rain falls, who was hit with the first drop? Impossible to say, but the thunder certainly sounded. Pistols and rifles were drawn and fired. Horses and men screamed as they careened together, an avalanche of flesh and lead.

They were so close that as each party rode into one another, the lines merged making it near impossible to tell in that first moment who was who.

Stoney flew past him. Porter drew his pistol and fired hoping to hit the lead robber but instead got one of Stoney's men, Arch, who took the bullet in the chest and head, and fell from his horse with a terrible cry upon his lips. Porter drew back on his reins and narrowly avoided getting shot from behind by a long mustachioed man called the Tartar.

Mary hit the Tartar and his horse equally with the blast from her shotgun. The horse reeled over, knocking the Tartar from the saddle. She dismounted and ran for cover in the trees along the steep side of the road as several of the Mountain Hounds drew guns, and one or two shot at her.

Someone ran into Jack's horse and he was thrown to the ground. His opponent tried to trample him, but Jack shot the horse. Man and beast tumbled down together.

Zeke and Boles had been riding a little farther behind the other three and were thusly in a better position to stop and fire at their antagonists.

Dawg wasted no time in recognizing the scent of his enemies, tearing a man from the saddle, then going after a second.

The man on the ground, Glasgow Red, was dazed, but hatred burned in his eyes and he drew a gun to shoot the dog.

Porter ended his plans with a well-placed shot between the eyes.

The Tartar was wounded but not nearly so bad as he looked, he reared up and lunged at Porter with a long Khyber knife. Reloading, Porter gave the long mustachioed man his boot.

Knocked back, the Tartar wiped blood from his nose and mouth and cried out, charging again with his blade held high for a killing stroke.

Porter leaned hard on the saddle just as his horse jerked away from the oncoming attack. He was flung to the ground and his horse galloped away. Nearly breathless, Porter lay on his back like a turtle under the blazing sun.

The Tartar screamed and slammed his blade at Porter's head burying it in the hard-packed ground a hairsbreadth from Porter's neck.

Porter dodged away and kicked, fumbling to get his cylinder to seat properly in his dragoon. The Tartar came again with his flashing blade. The cylinder sat and Porter cocked the hammer, letting it rain flame and flying death across the Tartar's frame.

The snarling white dog in their midst made several of the Mountain Hounds horses panic and throw their riders along with the crazed fury of black powder and lead.

Stoney wheeled his horse about to face Porter but glanced at the foes behind him. He dismounted and stepped to the low side of the road for cover amongst the trees. He fired at the two men farther away before turning back to look for Porter.

"I'll kill you, Brown!" cried Stoney.

Mary took a shot at him but missed.

Porter shot a man before him and the other leapt from his horse to gain cover from the beasts, but Dawg had other ideas.

A bullet whizzed angrily past Porter's head like a wasp. It came from Stoney, not more than fifty paces away, nestled beside a thick pine. He fired at Stoney, but the big man ducked back into the thick brush.

Mary hit a snaggle-toothed man in the leg, he cried out and fell from his horse.

Zeke and Boles took careful aim, both shooting at Stoney who they recognized as the architect of their woes. But as he had for Porter, Stoney vanished back into the greenery.

Jack found himself face to face with the snaggle-toothed Leeds, both men had been thrown from their horses and were wrestling with pistols drawn. The snaggle-toothed man fired several times towards Jack's head, but his aim was off, hitting the dirt next to Jack. A ricochet from the ground wrenched into Jack's shoulder. But the gun firing beside his head seemed worse. The explosion of black powder beside his ear made Jack scream in pain until he was deaf, but he never ceased his grip with the foe. He wrenched the man over and finally struck him in the mouth with the butt of his own gun, ending the struggle.

Cleve, the second in command to Stoney, was the last of the Mountain Hounds still on his horse. He fired wildly and tried to break from the close melee and gain a new position.

Mary shot at him with the Sharps but missed.

Cleve charged headlong toward Zeke and Boles, and still firing, struck Zeke square in the chest. The bullet ripped out his back.

Zeke looked confused as a wash of bubbling crimson ran down his chest. "Hey. That wasn't supposed to happen." He pitched over on his face, dead.

Boles stood fast and fired within only a few feet but missed his quarry, who fired back and got him in the shoulder. Boles cried out in pain, dropped his gun, and scrambled to escape, crawling on his hands and knees back behind a pine.

Emboldened by his killer success even though his pistol was out of ammunition, Cleve kicked his horse after Boles, urging the stallion to trample the little man who crawled fast like a dog around the tree, crying out for help.

Reed had been pulled from the saddle by Dawg and knocked senseless for a moment. That had saved his life as Dawg paid him no more attention once he no longer struggled. Once he awoke, he was shooting again, though without any degree of accuracy.

Porter finished Reed with a well-placed shot, then focused back on Stoney and Cleve far back toward Boles and Zeke.

"They killed Zeke," shouted Mary, as she took another shot, but missed again. "I'll use my knife!" she cried as she ran toward Cleve with her bowie knife.

Cleve was well aware of Mary's bloody reputation with a knife, she had killed at least four mestizos with it. He quickly reloaded a cylinder in his own gun.

Stoney sprang from his cover and shot at Mary, and she narrowly dodged away, taking cover on the other side of the road once more.

Cleve took a moment from pursuing Boles and shot back toward Mary, making her dive behind another tree for cover.

Spicer had been another victim of Dawg, and though he had a bloody leg, his falling horse had chased the animal away and left him to recover his wits and get back in the fight. He shot at Porter, forcing him to dismount and take cover beside a fallen horse. Behind him, a panicked horse whinnied and ran back toward Coloma.

Porter tried to get a bead on the man but was unable. Dawg, however, remembered his foe and crept up from behind and took care of Spicer by the jugular.

Cleve renewed his interest in killing Boles and charged after the man who had run away twenty paces to another tree before tripping in the underbrush and tumbling to the ground.

Boles got up in a panic. His shoulder wound had already soaked half of his shirt with blood. He tried to escape in another direction, hiding beside a thick pine that had most of its lower branches sheared off, but Cleve rode around the other way cutting him off with a devilish grin.

"Time to die, Bart," said Cleve with terrible finality as he brought his pistol to bear and fired. Bark exploded from the tree just a few inches from Boles face. "I'm gonna piss on you again when you're dead."

"No, sir!" said Boles, though it came out more like a shriek. "I'll piss on you! You fine haired sons of bitches!"

Cleve shot but missed as Boles ducked away. Cleve urged his horse on after the small man.

Boles jumped back the opposite way and Cleve wheeled his horse about, intent on killing the seemingly helpless foe. As Cleve reined hard to the left, his horse reared against the soft ground and sent Cleve's chest into a broken branch. The jagged end sheared right through his ribcage and Cleve was snagged from off his horse's back. Pinned to the tree, the branch pierced his lung. He hung there with his boots kicking at empty air, surely the longest three seconds of his life, until the dry branch snapped, and he hit the ground, drowning in his own blood-filled lung.

If there was any life left in Cleve at that point, Boles kicked it out of him. Then Boles kept his word and dropped his trousers to give the dying man an inglorious taste of urine. "Yes sir, you tell them Black Bart Boles sent you to hell with a mouthful of piss!"

Porter glanced at Jack. "You all right?"

"What?" called Jack. "I can't hear anything."

Porter nodded to him. "Dawg!" he called, and Dawg came loping toward him, fresh red across his muzzle. He was still hurt and couldn't run as fast as he used to, but his dedication to Porter was undaunted.

Mary pointed toward Boles who was standing over the dead body of Cleve. "That's all of them except Stoney."

They could hear a light racket of a man running away through the thickets. "Sounds like he is making a run for it back to Coloma through the mud."

A couple of shots were fired from out in the gathering dark but were not even close to reaching them.

Porter declared, "I'm going after him."

"I'm coming with you," Mary said. "We must get the key."

Porter snagged his horse's reins. "They got Zeke, and Jack is wounded and deaf. I need you to help them gather the horses and get back to the Round Tent."

"You need back up," she protested.

"I have Dawg."

"He is still wounded. I'm not."

Porter mulled that over.

Jack shouted, "I'm alright. I can get Zeke and head back with the horses. You go get the son of a bitch!"

Boles trotted toward them. His shirt was a wretched smear of blood. "Fellas, I don't feel so good." He collapsed before them.

Porter rushed to his side and examined his wound. "He got hit in the arm, lost a lot of blood. He might make it." He tore off Boles sleeve and wrapped it around his shoulder. "Mary, help me get him on a horse."

The two of them lifted Boles onto a horse and he came to, blinking awake. "Where am I? My arm hurts. Where's Zeke?"

Porter took hold of Boles' belt and wrapped it about the saddle horn. "Hold on, you gotta keep alive long enough to help Jack get you patched up."

Jack stood and held the reins of another horse. "I got this!" yelled Jack. "Go get Stoney!"

"You're hit yourself."

"What?" Jack shouted.

Porter shook his head and pointed at Jack's shoulder.

Jack shouted, "It just grazed me. I'm alright except for being deaf!"

Porter nodded at him and signaled him to grab as many horses as he could. Jack acknowledged him.

"I'll get Zeke back home. What about the rest of these fellers?"

"They can feed the crows."

BLACK WINGS

Far back up the mountainside, just as the darkness revealed the torch fires of beyond that we call stars, a cosmic movement signaled that the conjunction was *right*. The veil between worlds was at its thinnest, and what might have seemed an infinite gulf between worlds and dimensions moments ago, was now separated by the barest thread of the ether.

An earthquake rumbled and a portion of the mountain sloughed off from itself in a deadly morass, revealing a gaping door not crafted by human hands. Amidst the debris of earth and stone was a scattered tumbling of massive bones. Near the place where the Chinese had found the Dragon Bones, a few small caves were revealed in the steep mountainside. A myriad of black winged bats swarmed out of these caverns, welcoming the newfound exits amidst the unholy rolling of the mountain—but they were not alone.

𝍫

Stoney saw that he was alone. He sent a few wild shots toward Brown and Mary, then ran back through the swampy area to get a head start on returning to his own encampment. He had just lost the last eight of his most devout followers. In just two days, the Mountain Hounds band which had been robbing and murdering throughout the California territory for the last four years, was no more.

He could always get more men and he would always hunger for revenge, but in the moment, he was outgunned. He had to think of the now, getting out alive and living to strike back another day.

He raced as fast as he could back across the muddy ground until he reached a boardwalk that led along a flume and took him back into Coloma. From there he stole a horse and rode hard the mile and half back to his hideaway.

He continually looked back over his shoulder to be sure Brown wasn't closing in on him. That he wasn't being followed. They had slain his men, but they had wounded and dead men, too. Difference being, he knew they would be waiting up on their wounded, that wasn't his problem anymore, he could travel light and fast, and only one thing mattered. No, two things, revenge and the strange copper book.

But revenge could come later, right now he just had to get back and lay his hands on the book.

Darkness was coming and the stars, which were right, were blinking awake. Why had that thought come to him? What made them *right*? Here and there the gleaming campfires of the miners cast hellish lights amidst the dark forest, and shapes pent in hell swirled awake.

Something akin to birds or bats flitted through the night sky. These black and gaunt forms swooped and dipped at one another like cascading whirlwinds. They drew ever nearer, and Stoney wondered if his eyes were playing tricks on him.

He could waste no more time with such fanciful thoughts, he knew Brown was coming and hell was coming with him.

He tied the horse behind his shack, guessing that a cursory glance wouldn't fool most anyone searching who might own the animal, but he was more than a mile from where it was taken and guessed he had a bit of time.

Stoney lit his oil lamp then gathered up his best gear and grabbed a belt and box with spare ammunition, caps and balls, and powder. He took a sack and tossed in a few vittles, jerky, hard tack, and even a few bruised apples. He took a couple bottles of whiskey that he had stolen from Porter's wagon the other night and put all of that in the saddle bags.

He was done with this place, but this strange book would make it all worthwhile.

Stalking back inside the shack, he moved his cot and a dirty frayed mat. From under those he pried up some loose floorboards and casually tossed them to the side of his shack. In the dirt was his squared treasure hole. He had a small bit of gold stashed therein along with an extra pistol. From the hole, he pulled up a burlap bag. The item inside was reasonably heavy for its size. It clanked as he returned the loose boards, then he opened the bag to gaze upon its wonder once again. He had been compelled to have it ever since, just two night ago, he'd gazed through a small hole in the Round Tent Saloon and saw the strange item. It wasn't even gold, but it captivated him like nothing else ever had. He couldn't explain it to himself, but he desired it more than he had wanted that pretty calico gal back in Sacramento, the redhead with the big bosom, the one he had spent so much coin on.

This peculiar copper book was not of this world as near as he could recollect. It called to him. He had been compelled to steal it, and for what? He didn't know, he was so taken by it. He opened the book and it slid open circular like a flower blossoming. It made a strange, star-like form, and the glyphs etched deeply into it seemed to dance and move in the weak lamplight. There were dozens of signs and wonders that he could not fathom the depth of their mystery, others looked like Egyptian and still others perhaps like some of the crude Cherokee he had seen when he was boy. Here and there were monstrous signs and evil looking wards.

He was taken aback at the sudden sound of horse hooves. How long had he been staring at the book? It had seemed mere moments, but he could tell instantly from the dying lantern with its oil guttering low it must have been longer than it felt.

"That's far enough, Stoney. Drop your guns."

It was Brown! How had he gotten here so fast? At least he was by himself. That made things fair, even though Stoney never played fair.

He withdrew his pistol and shot toward the dark figure on horseback. But he was night blind from staring at the book with the lantern's glow across the copper face.

Brown returned fire and a bullet ripped through Stoney's arm. His arm was soaking wet with hot blood.

"I said drop it! Last chance, ya Puke!" cried Brown.

Stoney knew this was it. Either he took the shot to end this threat or met his fate at the end of a rope—that was no way for a man like him to die. He went to raise his pistol but realized it was no longer in his hand, he held only the book. His wounded arm had held the pistol. The gun was on the ground at his feet.

Confusion washed over him. He was losing a lot of blood and his thoughts were clouded and heavy.

A sudden gust of wind blasted him in the face, and he heard Brown shooting, but the crack shot missed! Stoney wondered why he wasn't being hit by the hot lead.

Strong, gaunt arms picked him up off the ground. Who else was here? Was it Bloody Creek Mary? She was strong as any man, but no, it couldn't have been her. The wind slapped him in the face, and he couldn't touch the ground. Who had him?

Bullets whistled angrily nearby but got rapidly farther away. He looked down and saw lean black arms holding him firm across the chest. The arms were darker than the Jamaican slave he knew when he was boy, what was his name? Something like Green? These arms were skinny for how strong they were. And darker than coal. Whoever it was, they had saved him from sure death at the hands of Brown and Bloody Creek Mary. They were a guardian angel.

He craned his neck back so he could look upon the face of this guardian angel.

The thing looking back at him had no face.

It was like a man merged with a bat's wings. It was the color of night and gaunt as skin wrapped over a skeleton. But even a skeleton would have had a face of sorts, this was a rounded mask of obsidian

Stoney screamed and scrambled to escape the clutching embrace of this night-colored being. He kicked and fought and bit and lost the precious book he had held in the crook of his good arm.

The night gaunt was immune to his struggles, but once it realized he had dropped the book, it screamed despite a mouthless face and dropped Stoney to pursue the falling book.

Stoney felt the ground rush up to greet him and he knew no more. The jumbled river boulders beside the road were less forgiving than even Porter.

ⅲ

"What the hell are those?" asked Porter, as he shot toward the second one swooping low to the ground ahead of them.

Bloody Creek Mary urged her horse to keep up with Porter's and even though she could only hear half of what was asked, she knew the question. "Ghost Horn called them Night Gaunts."

The first one that had held Stoney swooped in a wide circle and flew back toward Porter like it was daring to meet him head on.

Porter put his reins in his teeth and drew a second pistol. With both guns trained on the head of the thing, he fired away, letting a prayer guide each ball of lead.

A dozen lead balls struck the diving Night Gaunt in its blank face. It careened into the road directly in front of them, causing his horse to rear in a panic. Porter regained control of his mount and drew up before the black thing in the road.

It hissed, and Porter let loose another volley into the thing before realizing it was the swift decomposition of the body creating the hiss, not the thing itself.

Like ice swiftly melting under a summer sun, the black thing hissed and bubbled as gray steamy vapors rose from the collapsing corpse. Within mere seconds, the bat-like body of the Night Gaunt was gone.

Porter and Mary glanced up to see the other Night Gaunt wheeling through the sky, the copper book in its clawed grasp.

"It's heading toward the mountain door. We must hurry." Mary kicked her heels into her horse, urging it after the strange being.

Porter glanced once more time back at the spot on the ground. Only a fading mist vaguely resembling the shape of the bat-like thing remained. There was no hint left of the monstrosity beyond that. Who would believe this?

Just a short distance away, Stoney's broken body laid on his back among the river rocks. He was splayed out facing the night sky, a look of utter horror frozen upon his face. At least he was dead for good this time, mused Porter.

THE DOOR INTO THE MOUNTAIN

Porter and Mary urged their horses up the trail past Williamson's as fast as they dared. The cold chill was matched only by the glint of the full moon. Porter was grateful that if they must make this arduous trek as swiftly as they could that the moon lit their path liberally.

Urging their frothing horses up the trail, they struggled past the spot where the Chinese had camped. Some sections of the trail had buckled from the earthquake. Porter had felt the tremor but not realized it was big enough of a shock to cause this kind of damage, but here and there were strange tears in the face of the mountain. All things considered, it was amazing that Williamson's flume was still going to capacity, it had hardly buckled and leaked at all, even with a gouge in the land forcing it to straddle a new ravine like a bridge.

Their horses made the leap across, and Porter was grateful it wasn't any wider than it was.

Almost to the spot where they had first met Slow Badger and talked with Ghost Horn, they heard a great, wailing sound.

The landscape had changed. Some parts of the forest were all turned on end, pointing at the moon as if it were the ten on a clock, and the mountain trail was widened from a mudslide that had carried away a vast chunk of ground creating a new plateau. The sound was the wailing of Indian women and children.

There was no sign of the tepee's or any other part of the small camp Porter had visited a night ago. With the utter change on the mountain, he wasn't even sure which way to look anymore.

Mary spoke to one of the women who gestured to the wide expanse of earth before them, then pointed just ahead.

"She says the quake killed most of the men, including Slow Badger, her husband."

Porter grunted, asking, "What about the…?" He couldn't even bring himself to use the words to describe the Night Gaunts, instead he swirled a finger in the air.

The woman rattled off a horrified answer and pointed at the mountain.

"She says they opened the door and went in," answered Mary.

"What?"

The devastation of the land had made them miss a new darkness that beckoned just to their right.

"I'll be dipped." Porter consciously shut his mouth as he gazed upon the dark doorway.

Cast like an open gate to the underworld, titanic doors twelve feet tall loomed open. They were each near enough to six feet wide and looked green with age, until Porter realized the doors were not corroded metal but seemed to be made from a marbled green stone, perhaps emerald? The threshold, what little Porter could see of it, was hewn from the mountain's living rock and marked with glyphs similar to what he'd seen on the book itself. A sloping path led into utter darkness.

"They went that away?" he asked, regretting the question.

"They did," came Ghost Horn's voice. The old man struggled forward from the slanted tree slope. "The Night Gaunt made it through the thinning of the veil and took the book back and opened the way for the Old Ones. The door must be shut again."

"So, lets push these doors shut and start backfilling it all," offered Porter.

"The doors cannot be shut unless we have the key," said Ghost Horn.

"We have to go in and get it back," said Mary.

Porter chewed at the edges of his beard. "I killed one of those things and it faded into mist. How many more are there?"

"The Night Gaunt are but few and the weakest of what you will encounter there."

Mary said something in a language Porter didn't understand, and Ghost Horn answered her in likewise fashion.

"Wait, you gotta tell me what's gonna happen if I don't do this. Cuz I don't fancy a trek into the dark with those things. What does it all matter?"

Mary answered, "The Sleeping Gods will awaken and come out again. They will bring death to the land like has not been

171

seen in thousands of years. The best we can do is put them back to sleep."

"How do we do that?"

"We take back the key and shut the door."

"You see, that part sounds simple, but I reckon it really ain't."

"It isn't, but it's the only chance we have."

Porter mulled things for a moment. "I trust you Mary, but can it really be as terrible as you say? Is this just gonna affect your people or what?"

"It will affect everyone. It will take time, but it will spread the world over, as they awaken more of their brethren sleeping in far off places—perhaps beneath the sea, or in the highest of mountains—but they will awaken all of the sleepers. And that will doom humanity."

Porter wanted to be dubious, to doubt all of these strange revelations, but he had seen too many things the last three days to deny that there was a whole lot more to the world than he had ever guessed before.

"How can just the two of us succeed?"

"Well," answered a new voice, "I'd say keep your powder dry and give them as much hell with that thunder and lead as you can. You've been doing alright so far."

Porter spun about to face the newcomer. It was the hoary old miner he had seen before a time or two. The old man had a thick bushy mustache and beard to match, along with eyes that twinkled bright in the firelight, almost phosphorus-like. Porter never had any reason to think the white-bearded man was a threat or up to anything, but the way the old man had suddenly appeared amongst not only Mary and himself, but Ghost Horn and the rest of the gathered Indians gave him pause. No one was that sneaky.

"Who are you, mister, and what do you know about all this?" asked Porter, suspiciously.

"Call me Mr. Nodens, if you like. I know a thing or two about these goings on. I like to keep tabs on the Old Ones and see that they keep to their own place."

Porter looked at him shrewdly, wondering if he was speaking with a mad man or a demon in human form.

Mr. Nodens continued, "I can see you're wary as a caged wolf, and that's a fine way to be considering these here strange things. After all, even I lost track of a couple of my hounds, and they went rogue and answered the call of another master. Glad you took the one down before I had to."

"Hounds?"

Mr. Nodens gave a soft sound like a chuckle, but declined any further answer on the subject, instead he went on, pointing at the gaping doorway. "Down there is a whole lot of pain and hurt, fear and madness. Don't be deceived, it's a real dark place despite any amount of light you might bring to it."

"What's down there?" demanded Porter.

"Slippery blasphemies," hinted Nodens with a wry smile.

"You got anything more to tell me? Something useful?"

Nodens gave a lopsided grin. "There are strange objects in the great abyss, and you ought to take care and not wake the sleepers. Truth is, I'd love to go with you, Porter, it could be a great hunt, but I'll have to settle for just putting you on the path tonight. I can't cross that threshold myself. Bad knees." He tapped at his legs.

"How do you know my real name?"

"I know lots of things that men don't, but for now, you'll have to trust me. Ghost Horn and the woman, they speak true. This infestation is gonna have to get cleaned out before it spreads."

"Well, thanks for that," said Porter, rolling his eyes to Mary. "But you haven't really told me anything."

Mary shook her head, warning Porter with, "We should abide his wisdom."

Porter faced Nodens. "Then share some wisdom I can use. Otherwise, I'm getting awful tired of the poetic inuendo and excuses."

Nodens grinned, nodded his hoary head, and reached his wizened hand forth. He took Porter's hand in his and clasped it firmly. "Keep this until your return."

Porter felt nothing but the old man's weathered palm, but as Nodens withdrew his hand, it left there a mystic light that danced like an aetheric flame. It rapidly grew until it was almost as large as Porter's hat. It resembled a wavy star. It gave no heat and minimal light but exuded a primal power.

Glancing up, Porter realized Mr. Nodens was gone. Swallowed by the infinite sea of blackness.

Ghost Horn nodded. "You are gonna need that."

Porter spun about, searching for Nodens. "Who was that?"

Ghost Horn shrugged. "He gives himself any name he wants, but we have always called him The Great Coyote. He is wily but a trickster, too."

"A trickster? And I should trust him on this?"

Ghost Horn said, "He doesn't want the Old Ones coming out any more than we do. We can trust him on that."

Porter wrinkled his nose. "And I'm supposed to trust this guy with a star light as I go into an abyss to get back a book to shut these doors?"

Mary took Porter's hand. "It must be done. This way must be closed off from the sleepers within. I will go by myself if you will not."

No way he'd let her go on alone. "Dawg, you're wounded so you're staying here." He pointed dramatically at the ground. Dawg watched his hand anxiously, then sat in the fresh earth beside Ghost Horn.

"Good thing I was loaded for bear already going after Stoney. I've still got a dozen cylinders on me, along with a pocketful of shells for the Sharps. Let's get this over with," he said.

Bloody Creek Mary said something softly to Ghost Horn. The old medicine man nodded.

"What was that?" asked Porter.

"He will sing the song of the Sasquatch. That we might get some help."

"What's a Sasquatch?"

"The furry people."

Porter's eyes nearly bugged out. "A song for them? And help? No, thanks."

Mary shook her head, but signaled to Ghost Horn, who began a droning chant and padded his hand on a skin drum.

The moon hid behind the clouds, and darkness seemed to envelope everything as they stood before the doorway. The doorway looked like a fang-toothed mouth with stalactites and stalagmites leering up and down. The forbidding aspect was palpable.

"Every journey needs a first step," said Porter, as he drew his pistol in his free hand. Mary clutched the shotgun with both hands. Porter held the bizarre wavy star light in his other hand a little high, then they walked in.

TRAILS IN DARKNESS

Porter and Mary crossed the threshold of the titanic doorway. The vibrating star in Porter's hand cast eerie light on the path before them. The path was made of rough basalt flagstones that were all joined in a non-linear pattern resembling nothing so much as fractals in broken ebon glass. It was readily apparent that this place was ancient as anything Porter had ever seen, granted he was the son of a young country, but this was beyond even those places of antiquity he had heard about in far off lands across the sea. This was a place made from another age beyond any he was aware of.

Ghost Horn's chanting song was the only thing Porter could hear as it echoed softly behind them, since the gaping tunnel before them devoured all sound and light.

"Ugh, this is gonna get uglier, before it gets better isn't it?"

"Is there any other way?" she answered.

"Is that a joke? Didn't think you had it in you."

"I don't," she said.

Porter grimaced, she really didn't have a sense of humor.

They walked on for some time. A few chunks of fallen rock and a peculiar bend in the sidewall revealed at their feet a gaping hole leading into utter darkness. The path continued on the other side of the hole. It wasn't difficult for them to circumnavigate the precipice, but the bottomless feel of the thing, along with a slight breeze wafting up at them, was disconcerting.

The tunnel slanted deep into the earth and Porter noticed that if there was just a little more dampness or a coating of dust upon the stones, it would be too slippery to walk back up. Boots were great for horses but hell for slickrock and caving. His bizarre light cast two dozen feet further where he saw an abrupt drop off.

"Hold up, let's get a rope here just in case," said Porter. They tied a firm knot and wrapped it around a thick stalagmite, then he made a wide knot on the end and wedged that against a nearby boulder that had fallen from the ceiling. He gauged it weighed more than he and Mary put together. They eased the full length of the rope down the slope.

"I'll go and take a look over the edge and see how far it goes. If it's bottomless, we're up a creek since this rope ain't much more than fifty feet."

Mary grunted her answer as Porter wound the rope about his waist and eased down the steep embankment. His boots skittered and slipped and if not for the rope he would have gone right over the brink.

"Might be we missed a secret turn or something," he suggested.

Mary glanced at her surroundings. "There might be another way back at the first drop off."

Porter peered over the edge, fully expecting to see nothing, like the bottomless pit earlier, but was pleasantly surprised to see that it was only about a seven-foot drop to the bottom where passing through a slightly smaller tunnel, the path went on.

"Come on down, we can keep going," he said. He let himself down nice and quick, then glanced into the tunnel beyond. The smaller aperture blasted wind in his face.

Mary eased herself down and readied the shotgun.

Porter stalked inside. The cavern opened to a wide, vast dominion. He could no longer see the roof of the subterranean world. The ground was flat and sandy instead of stone, and they saw their own light glinting on the silver surface of a lake not more than five paces away.

"Might be a lake now, but this sandy shore tells me it might occasionally flood and carry sediment higher, maybe that's what broke through the wall we just came through," Porter said.

The walls beside them were cliff-like, rising almost vertically with few enough cracks, seams, or points gouging out into the darkness.

"How can we even know if we're on the right path? Those flying demons might just as well have gone down the pit we saw earlier as come here."

Mary swung about looking in every direction. "They probably connect up there somewhere. It would all lead to the heart of the mountain and the abyss—where they sleep."

"You're saying we should press on, not knowing where we are going?"

"It's this way," she said, taking the lead, despite Porter holding their only light.

He followed closely on her heels, ever mindful of all the strange tricks of light the glittering star in his hand cast upon the blue-black rock.

"Might have been nice for old Ghost Horn or Mr. Nodens to tell us something useful to do in this situation. Are we expecting to just see that demon bat thing sitting and taking a read with the gold book or what? It's not like he'll just hand it over to us."

"Shhh," urged Mary as she paused and stared into the deep gloom.

She remained still a long time, and after a long minute Porter moved in closer and whispered into her ear. "What do you see?"

"Nothing. But the blackness moved, I could sense it."

"Maybe you ought to let me get in front with the light then."

"No," she insisted. "Better that I should douse it somewhat."

They trekked on over the hard-packed sand. Every now and again, Porter would wheel and look behind. The massive gallery of a cavern and the impenetrable dark played havoc with his senses and he wished Dawg was there, but it was not a good place for a wounded four-legged animal to be moving in.

The sound of rushing water met their ears, but it was a much longer walk to the waterfall than they expected. The cavern both hushed its sound and strangely echoed it deafeningly once they were almost on top of it.

"I do believe by now we are under an entirely different mountain."

"It's the same," said Mary. "Our trail has simply taken us around the far side of the lake."

Porter tried to get his bearings right and either confirm or dispute Mary's assertion, but he could do neither. It was a bizarre feeling for the frontiersman, he was usually the one with the best sense of direction. Of course, despite all his time living the way he had, he was still infinitely more civilized than Mary was, she'd been raised in this wild country as had her ancestors for centuries untold. He had to admit that her connection by blood to the land was deeper than his could ever dream of being.

"You know where we are in relation to getting out? And I do mean quickly if we have to. I don't understand how this star is still lit. I don't know how much more oil it can hold."

Mary gave a half-smile. "It's not oil and it won't burn out. It is the old magic and will burn so long as you hold it free."

"Forever?" he asked dubiously.

She nodded. "But Nodens will ask for it back when the job is done."

Porter stared at the strange wavy star. It had a glow circling around it, and he could see glyphs floating in the golden haze moving ever so slightly like words traveling down a river. It reminded him of characters he had seen in what seemed ages ago, when his best friend in all the world had shown him some curious characters of a lost and arcane era. He shook himself free of the moment, remembering the dire straits they were in here and now.

Mary, as if she had been waiting for Porter to focus, said, "We are across the lake from the exit we came in. If we had a canoe, we could return faster."

"I don't see a canoe down here, do you?" said Porter.

"There," she pointed.

Porter peered into the gloom and saw the slight curve of a rock near the silvery waters of the lake. He approached it cautiously and saw that it was indeed a canoe of curious workmanship. It was wood and looked seaworthy, though the design was not familiar to any he had seen before. It looked neither made by white men or any Indian tribe. It had a long flat bottom and a pair of oars, but the manner it was constructed was entirely alien.

"Well, I don't know how it got here, but looks like it could carry us both across the great deep, if you think that's the best way to go when we're done here."

"I don't know," she said. "We must now find the place where they sleep."

"They?"

"The Old Ones. The book will be beside them somewhere close. We must hurry before they wake."

"Won't that bat thing just wake them?"

Mary shook her head. "We must do what we can."

Porter grimaced and followed her. He didn't like feeling out of his element, out of control. Mary didn't know a lot of things about the way of the world he came from, but she seemed to know a whole lot more about this strange and weird world than she had ever let on in the last couple months she had worked for him. He always thought he was doing her a favor by taking her in when she was half dead and covered in blood. He soon realized it wasn't her blood, but that of the half dozen mestizos she had killed who had murdered her family. It's a hard world and he knew what it was like to lose people close to you, and he would have done the same as her. But she had narrowly survived and only too soon after she had done the deed, it looked like the local miners had wanted to string her up for murder. It had taken a lot to get everyone to back down. Only some of the Mountain Hounds had protested, saying the mestizos were friends of theirs and must have been jumped by Mary's clan. But no one believed that. The mestizos were usually shot on sight by any of the Spanish ranchers, and no one would miss them.

Now he wondered if she hadn't done *him* the favor, sticking around and helping out. He wasn't sure he could have run as lucrative a place without her and Jack. Now here she was leading the way into gripping darkness as they approached a roaring waterfall.

"It lies beyond there. It is the final doorway," she said.

"We gotta go through that?"

She nodded. "You must lead with the star."

Porter was skeptical but strode toward the falling white water. The star light gleamed on the opposing whiteness of the water that contrasted so strongly with the black firmament encompassing the rest of the cavern.

As he neared the waterfall, stepping upon the smooth flat rocks, he noted that they did resemble a path of flagstones akin to those from the upper entrance. He steeled himself, fully prepared to be drenched in the cold water—the spray from it was chilling—but the falls began to part like a drawn curtain before the power of the glowing star.

Porter gasped.

Beyond was a new cavern, deep blue lights revealing the outline of incredible citadels and towers of magnificent size. A city of fantastic antiquity lay spread there, held in mysterious, silent awe.

DWELLERS OF THE DEAD CITY

They stole forward, eyeing their surroundings, watching for any sign of life, and awed by the stark wonder of the seemingly dead city.

Statues of monstrous figures of titanic shape and girth held an archway leading deeper inside. All was thrown back from the clutching darkness, but the light was cold and unwholesome. Cyclopean pillars of tremendous size held up the roof of the mountain hall. Giant steps half as tall as Porter and each as wide as a street led to a palace marbled with jet or obsidian. Curling lines of rusted metal formed pathways all over the flagstones, and Porter wondered if each was like a guideline for some inhuman probe. It was maddening, and he wondered at who or what had created such a place only to leave it shrouded in darkness deep in the earth. Lost to the ages.

"Why is this here?" he said aloud, his words echoing in the vast chamber.

"Nodens said it was locked up and made for them to sleep."

"But why? And what happens when they wake?"

"We don't want them to ever wake," she said.

Staring at the lofty heights, Porter wondered how this place even remained hidden beneath the mountain they were in. It seemed too large in his mind's eye, as if it should be leering above the snow-capped peaks.

"Let us hurry and find the book." Mary tugged on Porter's jacket and pulled him along as he stared in wonderment at the bizarre spectacle.

Everywhere were deep cut glyphs and signs representing things he vaguely recollected he had seen on the pages of the book. The many parapets and towers, while set in a style differing from anything Porter had heretofore ever seen, did have some semblance to the fantastic real world he had dreamed about while listening to others read aloud tales to amaze. Here and there, gargoyles were perched atop protruding corners or lofty obelisks.

Then he saw one move.

As they strode across the wide forum, the creature which had remained still most of their intrusion, subtly shifted its weight and turned slightly to continue facing them, not unlike how a pigeon might adjust its perch. But this would more closely resemble a pigeon from hell

"Mary," Porter whispered through clenched teeth. "One of those damn bat things is up there watching us. Might be the same one that took the book."

Mary, whose culture was not subtle, wheeled about to look.

The Night Gaunt took to the air and swooped down at them. It was not carrying the book.

"No," urged Mary, but it was too late.

Porter fired his dragoon, the gun blazed red fire in the gloom and lead shattered the faceless horror of the Night Gaunt, splitting it wide open. It struck the flagstones and fizzed and hissed as it turned to an eerie mist.

"That wasn't so bad," said Porter.

"But now we risk the sleepers being awakened," she said.

Porter kicked at the roiling sulfurous murk. "I didn't see a way around it. You saw one of those things drop Stoney on his head, and I wasn't gonna let that happen to us."

Mary shook her head in frustration and pointed toward the bizarre temple structure ahead of them. "I just hope they are still imprisoned and asleep."

They hurried on, the sound of their boot leather slapping against the flagstones seemed terribly loud now in the echoing hall.

Jutting towers held the ceiling aloft and the strange features of the silent city beckoned them on.

Porter glanced in every direction, hoping the star light in his hand would catch any hint of movement or the gleam of any eye. Then he reminded himself that the Night Gaunt had no eye nor any face for that matter, what other horror might be down here lurking in the myriad shadowy corners?

Some of the deeply recessed glyphs caught the light from the star and seemed to flicker a moment as if gas had been struck and a wick was lit, but whenever he looked again, they remained cold and dark as the grave.

Mary had to swing a leg up to gain the first of the gargantuan steps that led into the temple. Porter himself was forced to holster his pistol as he could not manage the titanic step without at least one free hand.

"You got any other ideas or revelations, now is the time to spill," Porter said as he waited for here to gain the step and watch his back.

"I have no words," she said. "I simply feel that we must go in and see if the book is within this place."

"Keep your eyes skinned and let me up the next step before you follow," he grunted.

They did this time and again simply to climb the leviathan stair, until they reached the top. Doors like those that led into the mountain were upon this temple. But these were open only a crack. Porter didn't think he could squeeze through but supposed Mary might.

"Let's see if we can't open it enough for both of us to get through before we commit to what is on the other side."

Mary nodded and took hold of the door, and each of them strained to pull it open a fraction. The huge doors gave with little enough effort and Porter was relieved that they did not creak but seemed well-oiled. Peering in, faint blue light cast from far above came down in slanted blades, illuminating tiny sections of massive sarcophagi. This place was enormous as well, stretching on farther than he could see with the simple light he held along with the overhead blue coming from who knew where. The air was stale but not unpleasant. He wondered if the lake and waterfall kept preservation qualities here, as he had seen no sign of any form of the usual cavern dwelling animals. There had been no sign of fungus either. This truly was a city of the dead, for, so far, there had been no living thing save for the terrible Night Gaunt.

Porter held the star as high as he could reach, letting its wavy white light stretch a little farther. Something glinted in the distance, and he hoped it was the book. They hurried toward the gleam but slowed when they saw that it was a golden brazier, cold as death.

"Should have known better, the book was green with verdigris and shouldn't shine like that," Porter whispered.

Mary nodded but said nothing more. She let her grip on the shotgun loosen and pointed the barrel toward the ground.

Porter was puzzled, she had kept it level and ready to fire the entire trek here.

She stared blankly ahead then spun and walked to their left. Porter followed, wondering at what could be done, how could they find this precious book within a dark city where mysterious sleepers might awaken at any moment.

"Hold on a second, Mary. Where you going?"

Mary walked straight ahead, unheeding of his plea.

Holding his pistol and starry light high, Porter hurried to her side. Not until they were almost on top of it, did the light reveal an onyx squared monolith. It was as big around as a wagon and twice as tall. More of the strange writing was etched into its face. Porter wondered at its purpose, was it a marker of old times or a history relating what this place was? Did it tell the fate of the world riddled across its pitted black surface?

Mary ran her fingers across the smooth black stone.

"What is it? Do you know something?" he asked.

"I know nothing," she said. "But something calls to me here, something asking me to knock and it will be opened." Her face was so terribly blank, standing out in stark contrast to even her usual unfathomable look. It looked more like something was reading her than the other way around.

Porter yanked her away from the black stone. It broke the spell.

She shook her head. "What happened?"

"You tell me. You dropped your guard and walked toward this black stone, started running your hand on it saying it was calling to you."

She stepped back from the stone and glanced all around. "Last thing I remember, we were walking toward a golden shine."

"Nothing but a big candlestick."

Mary looked about in every direction.

"Whatever it is, don't let it take hold again. We should get out."

"I'm alright. We still must get the book. It's this way." She led him in the opposite direction.

Porter was wary as a hunted wolf, but at least this time she kept the scattergun up and ready, not relaxed like before.

The crack of the doorway, a wide blue line behind them several hundred yards, Porter kept his eyes on it as directional force. It stood out like a beacon versus the all-powerful wash of midnight that pervaded the chamber.

"Here," said Mary.

On a colossal dais of smooth black marble nearly ten feet high, sat the book, opened in its circular fashion. Behind it leered a wide screen not unlike a filmy window, but the greatest window of any age.

If Porter had not been positive he was standing upright with the world centered down at his feet, he might have thought he was looking into a monumental reflecting pool of dark water. But this stretched upright at more than forty-five degrees.

Looking again, he saw that it was transparent, but his eyes had not been ready for what was behind the wall of glass.

Beings were lined up there, like tin soldiers in a display box, yet these tin soldiers were each and every one of them at least twice as tall as Porter. They were all giants and wearing the most peculiar clothes of ancient fashion. Most had red hair and pale grayish skin. Some had jewels or golden tiaras or even wide sashes with the semi-familiar glyphs seen upon the book's plates denoting some title or brotherhood. There were men and women, all appearing roughly the same middle age, for they were all mature and he saw no children nor anyone appearing gray or elderly among them. Row upon row behind the glass, they appeared not dead but asleep.

"Are they sleeping?" he asked.

"So say all the legends," Mary answered.

"We better get that book and get the hell out of here in a hurry, I think. I'm done with this place, whatever the hell it is."

"I can't reach it." Mary strained for a foothold on the huge dais. She tried again to climb up and reach the book but slipped free.

"Allow me." He holstered his gun, and, with one hand, tried to give her a boost to climb the smooth stone and reach the book. He strained and lifted her as high as his shoulder, where she placed her foot and tried to leap, only to come tumbling back, taking him down to the flagstones with her.

"If we had kept my rope, I could have lassoed it."

Mary frowned. "Can you try and throw me higher?"

"For you to catch hold of what? Besides the book. Don't want you coming back down and breaking a leg down here."

"You catch me."

"Throw you and catch you, while I'm holding this here starry spook light? Don't know that I can do all that."

"We need to try something."

Porter scratched at his temple and peeled off his hat to wipe his brow. He glanced about for anything that might be of use. "Maybe that golden candelabra?"

Mary wrinkled her nose.

Porter strode to the thing and tried to see how it might be attached to anything at all. It was hanging on a chain suspended from heights he could not see.

The chain was a soft metal, and Porter pried at it single handedly for a long moment until he reached the star closer. The chain snapped as if it were wax and the star had melted it free. It hit the flagstones with a loud clang, and the hanging chain spun upwards as if it had been held by a weight and was now free and recoiling. The sound echoed throughout the vast chamber.

"I hope that wasn't some kind of alarm," he said, glancing back at a frowning Mary.

He picked up the brazier and rushed back to the dais that still held the book out of reach.

A grating sound came from somewhere in the cold distance.

A hushed red light appeared at the far end of the chamber.

"What is it?" Porter asked.

Mary shook her head, snarling urgently, "Do whatever you were going to do so we can get the book and get out!"

Porter nodded and tossed the brazier at the book. It smacked the edge of it, only succeeding in knocking it farther onto the middle of the dais. He caught the brazier as it came back down and tried again, this time he missed the book entirely and failed to catch it on its return fall on the other side where it clanged against the stones again.

A bizarre sound came from where they saw the reddish hued light. The rolling thunder reminded Porter of a flashflood, choked with broken tree limbs, rolling through a slot canyon.

"Good thing you didn't throw me," grated Mary, as she took the brazier and tossed, but it did no better than when Porter had done it. This time the brazier remained stuck on top of the dais beside the book.

Porter snorted. "You were saying?"

"What is that sound?" She turned toward the reddish light and aimed her shotgun toward the oncoming sound.

"Hell, if I know. We better split!"

"The book!" she insisted.

"Do we need this book no matter what? At the cost of our own lives?" he argued.

"Of course!"

"All right," Porter growled. "Since the alarm is already sounded." He drew his pistol and took aim.

THE SLEEPERS AWAKEN

Porter shot chunks of the marble away and bullets ricocheted and whistled off into the far reaching dark. One of the lead balls flew wide and struck the glass. It did not shatter but rippled as if the smooth incline were a limpid pool— albeit one resting at an impossible angle.

The book danced from the shots he fired and then fell forward. Mary caught it and ran toward the crack of a door.

Porter glanced at the giant figures sleeping behind the glass. The ripple on the glass continued to reverberate. He centered on a sleeping man dead ahead of him. A magnificent hulking specimen with a flaming red beard and golden crown, glyphs on the sash he wore resembled nothing so much as dragons and oriental characters. The red-bearded man behind the screen opened his eyes. Pale yellow light shone forth from the wide sockets like the furnace of hell.

Porter stumbled back; his heart jumped to his throat by this monstrous surprise.

The great slapping sound of the other danger suddenly became more imminent and Porter tore his gaze away from the shining one's eyes. The sound of rolling thunder grew nearer, and Porter glanced that way in wonderous fear. Light from the star in his hand cast strange movement but it was indistinct and wild, casting no semblance of life known to man. It did appear to be a like a flashflood or wave, and yet it was not spreading thin like water, but remaining in one singular mass as high as a man on horseback and yet as wide as three wagons apace. There was no conceivable way water should stay held together like that.

"I'll be dipped," said Porter, as he prepared to run.

Mary was already moving and almost to the crack of a door.

Porter glanced over his shoulder. The rolling flash flood was gaining on him. He wasn't sure he could make it to the door before it hit, and even if he did, the power of the water would blast those doors off their hinges, wouldn't they? A million thoughts raced through his head. If it was just water, why did he feel like it was coming for him, despite the fact it should be pouring out evenly throughout that great wide chamber?

He wondered about that red-headed giant that had opened its blazing eyes on him. What had it really seen? Was it sending this flood after him?

Mary passed through the cracked doorway.

"Close the door!" Porter shouted at Mary.

Mary shut one half solidly, thudding as it struck the threshold.

He glanced back; the tumbling wave of water was closing in. Were his eyes playing tricks on him? It almost looked like it had eyes opening and looking at him as it tumbled over itself, coming for him. Worse, black patches resembling toothy mouths snapped open and shut, too. He wondered if the room was filled with gas causing hallucinations.

He was almost to the door.

Mary glanced; her eyes wide with horror. She shut the door.

Porter reached the closed door and wheeled to face the wave. He held the star high, wondering what would happen to its light if a wave submerged it.

The wave stopped abruptly just a few paces from him.

It was not water.

A myriad of eyes and mouths opened and moved across the gelatinous body of the thing. Enormous and without solid form or shape, here and there at the edges a portion would probe forward along the lines of the flagstones, like water might, but then it would slink back to its greater body.

Porter was both disgusted and marveled by the thing. "You the guard dog?"

There was no response.

Porter knocked behind him at Mary. "Mary, if you're there, I'd appreciate you opening the door. I don't want to take my eyes off this thing."

"You're alive?" she asked timidly.

"For now. Open the door if you will please."

Mary pushed it open a crack. "You are Big Medicine."

Porter stared at the thing. "If you're the guard dog, I'm hoping you'll just stay. Stay!" he commanded, then slipped through the door and pushed it shut.

Mary asked, "What was that?"

"I was hoping you could tell me that Ghost Horn had a name for it, too."

She shook her head, eyes wide.

"We got the book, let's get the hell out of here!" They rushed to the steps and leapt down to the first one.

"Porter! Look!" Mary pointed back to the sill of the door. The slimy, semi-transparent creature was easing itself under the door, like a leaking basin.

"I told that thing to stay!" growled Porter as they hurried down the steps. It was a lot faster going down that it had been coming up.

They reached the bottom and Porter held the star up as high as he could. Slime or water caught the light at the top of the steps, running down in gleaming rivulets.

"We probably don't have much time, let's get moving. It came awful fast the first time."

They raced through the dark city, eyes up, watching for anything like the Night Gaunt again, but they saw nothing. The still blackness filled their senses and they looked back several times, chuckling nervously—their way of dealing with the maddening horror.

The roar of the waterfall was just ahead.

"I think we made it," gasped Porter. "No sign of the wave."

"We have to hurry. I still feel it calling to me to return the book. The power tugs on my mind."

Porter nodded and urged her on.

As they reached the waterfall, Porter held the star aloft and the waters drew back like a curtain once more.

"Is it still coming after us?" asked Mary.

"I can't tell and don't want to find out, let's hurry." Porter led them through the opening of the waterfall. There was a distinct difference in the air between the dark city and the mysterious lake. It still felt wrong and unwholesome, but they'd at least moved outside the pallor of the cold blue lights.

They crossed over and found themselves before the massive lake once more, the flagstone path gone, replaced by the sand covered shoreline.

The sand eased under their feet. Porter wheeled about, glancing toward the waterfall. There was no sign of the slimy thing they had seen earlier, but now that they had a waterfall behind them and a running stream into the lake would he even see it coming?

Porter tripped over something in the sand and turned back. Puzzled, he glanced down. There had not been anything on the strand when they had come this way the first time. A fist-sized stone lay there, then it abruptly twisted back and forth. Was it a crab, he wondered? He realized with horror that it was fist-sized because it was a fist.

The fist splayed its fingers forth in all directions like a man reaching for help. It rose from the wet sand and a whole arm to the elbow was revealed.

Waving the light all about them, Porter realized a multitude of gray limbs were rising. Several wretched faces rose above the sand, all of them crowing and gnashing their teeth.

"Back to the daylight!" cried Mary.

She shot at one, obliterating it, but before she could run, a dozen more burst from the sand.

"Eat lead!" shouted Porter as he fired at the sprouting horrors. He spun about shooting at them in all directions.

Something snarled and grasped for Mary's leg.

She swore in a native dialect and Porter's eyes flared in wrath as he shot the head from the ghoulish fiend as it tore itself free of the sands perilously close to sinking those teeth into her calf.

Farther back from Porter's rain of lead the ghouls were fully atop the strand, they rushed forward.

Mary reloaded the shotgun and loosed both barrels at the nearest ghouls, tearing them asunder.

With each blast of lead, the ghouls cringed, but they only ceased their resurrection if shot in the head.

Mary learned too late that multiple shots to the heart and chest did nothing to slow the terrors down. One lunged at her with half its body blasted away.

Porter brought his gun barrel to its forehead just before it clamped teeth down on her arm.

"There's an awful lot of these," growled Porter as he swiftly reloaded.

Mary swung the scattergun like a club, as she had no time to reload before the drooling corpses assaulted her.

Porter's shots rang out, rumbling in the massive cavern like a thunderhead ready to burst.

He kicked at a gibbering ghoul as it launched itself at him. The thing had little agility and went face first into the sand.

Porter shot the back of its head then brought his dragoon up just in time to slay another.

"Way too many, lets get to that canoe!"

He shot another six and urged Mary to the canoe as he tried to reload. It was difficult as the starry light in his left hand made the use of his palm impossible.

They ran across the dark beach. More of the unholy things rose with every footfall.

Mary reached the canoe first and pushed it into the still waters.

Porter reloaded and turned to shoot another half-dozen of the closest ghouls. Six dropped with split heads but another dozen were right behind them.

Mary grabbed an oar and rapidly paddled.

Porter leapt into the canoe. The canoe hit bottom from his added weight. It was stuck.

"Damnit!" He turned just as one of the ghouls reached the water's edge. Its eyes bulged, its tongue hanging out its agape mouth. Bile hung in long strings from its trio of teeth, the only teeth it had. Its clawed hands grasped Porter's jacket, its talons tearing holes into the lambskin.

Mary whipped the oar high and brought it down on the ghoul's head with a bone-crunching smack that nearly popped its eyes out. The thing fell into the waters, its body nudging the canoe farther out, just enough that the canoe slid free from the murky bottom.

"Reload! I have this!" ordered Mary, as she took both oars and plowed into the black waters with everything she had.

They skirted a few more feet from the shoreline, just as more of the ghouls' flabby feet splashed in. Several of them waded into the dark water up to their waists trying in vain to grab the canoe.

Porter fumbled with another cylinder as more ghouls splashed toward them. One of them dipped beneath the surface like a swimmer as the other two farther back seemed to give up, still gibbering their mad cry. Porter snapped in a cylinder and brought it up just as the head of the swimmer bobbed up beside them, a clawed hand grasped the side of the canoe, tipping it dangerously to one side. Porter leaned hard the opposite direction. The ghoul's puckered red mouth was leechlike.

Porter pulled the trigger and turned the fiend's head into fish bait.

Mary strained at the oars and they sped away into deeper water.

Back on the shoreline more than two dozen of the ghouls watched them speed away across the water. Some of them devoured their fallen comrades. They pranced like maniacs on the dim shoreline, then paused their crazed antics and rapidly fled in all directions.

"What is it?" asked Mary as she still pressed at the oars.

Porter answered, "Don't know, but I'm guessing that big wave of slime scared them off."

"Can you see anything?'

"Not yet, just that they all scattered," he answered.

Then Porter saw it, a glistening coming through the far darkness, the gelatinous bulk rolled over itself following their trail over the sand, heedless of the dead ghouls. The massive blob stopped at the water's edge, extended a few tendrils of itself high into the air and some low into the water. Apparently finding the answer to its questions, it poured itself into the dark murk with nary a splash, and Porter breathed, "Awww shit."

"What?" snapped Mary, panting hard from her exertions.

"We gotta speed this up," said Porter urgently. "You take the starry light. I'll row."

"I can't. It was given to you alone."

Porter clenched his teeth and stared back at the place where the thing had slid into the water. He couldn't see much of anything back across the lake anymore. They were too far into the black of the vaulted space, but there did seem to be a disturbance in the water. Beyond the stretching triangular break of the canoe, there was a slight rippling like something large was driving beneath the surface, causing a surge in their wake.

This was a bad place, in the water, in the dark, on a rickety little boat with a massive shapeless horror coming at you from unseen depths.

Mary grunted hard; she was giving this her all.

Porter hadn't shot and hit the thing yet, but its alien morphing bulk didn't bely something that appeared vulnerable to lead. It had at least halted its attack when he held the star up to it, maybe it could work again. Doubts crept in though, regardless the thing was still coming for them. What could stop it? The only thing that came to mind was fire, but he didn't have any on account of this starry witch light being their torch.

The swell following them was gaining.

LAST RITES

A sudden lurch forward sent them tumbling to the wet shore. Porter grappled with the edge of the canoe and murky water. He stood and glimpsed the surge in the lake coming at them fast.

"Which way is the exit?"

"This way," said Mary, already hurrying down the shore to their left.

Porter quickly followed.

Like a cat, Mary raced ahead of even Porter's light, she knew where she was going. Perhaps she could sense the breath coming from the small cave entrance.

At least this part of the strand wasn't crawling with ghouls.

Glancing back, Porter saw the great rubbery bulk of the slime monster begin to cover the canoe. He heard the wooden sides of the craft snap under the weight of the blubbery thing, then it was silent as the thing completely enveloped it. Stalks not unlike a snail's eyes sprouted from its gelatinous body and rapidly probed this way and that for a moment and Porter knew it sensed them.

Gunfire ripped Porter's attention away from the monstrosity.

Mary cried out and rapidly fired across the sandy beach at things Porter could not yet see.

Gray shapes shambled forth, gibbering hungry nonsense. Porter couldn't see their faces yet, but he could see their teeth gleaming.

He shot at the nearest few ghouls and they dropped, but more came swiftly behind those forward scouts.

"Where is that door?"

Mary hurried ahead only a few paces. "Here," she cried, ducking the low passage and vanishing into the dark.

He was mighty glad she had the confidence she did to keep moving in the dark.

More of the ghouls poured along the edge of the sandy beach. The splashing of their feet in the lake told Porter there were a lot more of them than he could see yet. Their mindless chattering was unnerving.

He ducked into the exit cavern and found Mary more than halfway up the rope they had left. He guessed it was a good thing they left it, instead of having it to lasso the book atop the dais.

It was only about seven feet high, but too far to jump and awful difficult for a man with a magical star blasting out of his left hand. He fretted trying to grasp the rope and climb. Scrambling behind made him turn with a raised gun.

Ghouls were in the tunnel mouth.

Porter shot each one that stuck its head within range. At the least the dead stopped up the small opening, gaining him a moment to again try his hand at the rope.

"Just hold and kick, I'll try and pull you up," said Mary from above.

"I'm too heavy for you and you're already tuckered from rowing, not to mention I know how steep that slope you're on is, you just get going. I'm a coming."

"No, you climb. I'll shoot anything that comes in behind you."

Something tore at one of the dead ghouls clogging the entrance.

Porter tried his hand at climbing the rope again. It was mighty difficult, he could only grip with his fingers, the bizarre starry light wouldn't allow him full purchase.

He was five feet up and almost over the lip when something tugged at his boot. One of the ghouls had Porter's heel full in its mouth. Porter kicked it back as Mary blasted it with the shotgun.

"How'd it get there so fast?" Mary asked.

"I think it was one of the ones you already shot and wasn't dead yet, just half of its face was gone."

Porter stepped over the lip and looked back as Mary hurried up the line. Ghouls were pouring into the bottom chamber. They glared up at Porter with open mouths and tongues wavering.

They were incapable of grasping the use of the rope and climbing after them, but Porter couldn't help but notice that despite that handicap, they kept climbing inside and crowding on top of one another. Soon enough they would reach the top of the tubular cavern and crawl after him.

He shot six more of them then reached for another cylinder and realized he didn't have any more.

A pile of gray scaly bodies tumbled over one another as they strained to reach the upper lip of the tunnel and pursue the human flesh.

Porter felt the tug of the rope as several of the ghouls pulled on it themselves in an effort to grasp their prey.

"Faster!" he cried, going up the steep slant as fast as his boots would allow.

The gibbering of the ghouls changed in tone to one that resembled panic, and then they went silent.

Curious, Porter looked over his shoulder.

The bodies of the ghouls, now entirely lifeless, were held together in a quivering mass as a clear gel seeped all around them.

"Aww wheat," he drawled. "Faster!" he shouted to Mary.

The bodies of the ghouls were tugged and suddenly ripped away into the larger cavern by the sticky mucous like tendrils of the blob.

Mary pulled herself up arm over arm until she reached the spot where they had fastened the rope. She drew a knife and slashed at the rope.

Porter took her by the shoulder saying, "Get to the door. The rope ain't gonna slow him down none."

She gazed down the end of the tunnel at the rising mass of gelatinous horror. Her eyes went wide with fear. "I thought it was the ghoul tugging on it!"

"It was," said Porter, urging her on. "He ate 'em. Let's get!"

They scrambled over the slick rock of the tunnel and over the chaotic rock and stalagmites that now seemed intent on barring their way and slowing them down.

The seething mass of the alien blob filled the passageway behind them like a rising flood.

"Hurry sister!" cried Porter, helping Mary up as she tripped over a jagged piece of basalt. Her legs were gouged and bloody from scraping across the rim on her secondary climb. She breathed heavily and sweat dripped from her face.

The cold light of the moon shone ahead, and they could hear the strange whistling chant of Ghost Horn outside as he still patted upon a drum and chanted the song of the Sasquatch, the furry people.

Porter half-carried Mary and they hurried together out into the night. Behind them, the welling of the terrible amorphous blob filled the passage.

"That monstrous thing is right on our heels!" shouted Porter. "Help us shut the door!"

"You still got my light I see," said Mr. Nodens, seemingly unconcerned about anything else.

"Yup," said Porter. "Thanks, it made things... interesting."

Mr. Nodens nodded and took the starry light from Porter's grasp. It shrank back down to the size of a matchhead, then vanished entirely.

"Much obliged you didn't lose it in there," said Mr. Nodens.

Porter shrugged. "If I had, I don't think I'd be here now. What about the door and that thing?"

"So shut it," said Mr. Nodens offhandedly.

Porter rushed to the door. Mary looked spent; she was still gasping for breath. But they each put their shoulder to the massive gate and strained at the great green doors but could not budge the titanic flaps. A huge shadow loomed behind them, blotting out the light of the moon. Porter turned to lock eyes with the giant wild man.

"I have sung to the Sasquatch, he is here to help," said Ghost Horn, alleviating sudden fears a fraction too late. Porter's hand was on his empty pistol, and he was glad to hear Ghost Horn's answer.

"Oh-Kay," said Porter, skeptical of the huge hairy man. But the Sasquatch, as Ghost Horn called him, stepped toward the doors and, taking hold of the massive edifice, shut the left-hand gate. There was a loud groaning and the doors gasped under the pressure, almost threatening to buckle from the force used by the wild man.

Inside, the gelatinous creature was almost to the door. Its probing tendrils reached a yard or more ahead of its swelling bulk, its eye-like pustules and open toothy mouths blinked and snapped before vanishing then reappearing at various places all over its insane body.

The Sasquatch took hold of the right-hand gate and strained to shut it as well. The bottom and top flexed from the power of the huge hairy man. Once closed the Sasquatch leaned its back against the door and held it as if expecting a battering ram.

Porter realized there was no way he could have forced the doors shut, not with the help of twenty men. He was glad the Sasquatch was here, even if it was an unnerving sight.

Ghost Horn continued his drumming and chant.

"The door is shut; we are back with the book. Now what?" asked Porter.

A terrible gong sounded as the gate itself flexed and bulged as it was battered by the thing inside the crypt. The Sasquatch was flung away but stood and renewed its efforts to hold the door shut.

Ghost Horn ceased his drumming and song, and looked to Mr. Nodens who said, "You have the key. But you must lock the door."

Mary quickly withdrew the book from her pouch. She opened it like a fan, turning it back into its spread flower-like configuration. She stared at the pounding door. The beating from the thing within shook the ground.

She looked at the door, then back at Porter with a creased brow. The Sasquatch strained, each strike from within sent it flying away. It would come back, looking a little more defeated each time.

Inspiration flew to his mind on majestic wings. "I think I know," said Porter.

"How?" she asked.

"I don't know how, just trust me." He took the book from her trembling hands.

He strode to the banging door and there, at about the midway mark, split between both doors, was a slight circular depression, the center of which looked the exact right size for the center latch of the book.

The Sasquatch looked pained as it tried to hold the door, it glanced down at Porter, with a look of worry and confusion.

"Hold on," he said to the Sasquatch. Porter snapped the circular book into the key like configuration. It went in but was not complete.

At his feet the jelly-like mass of the thing behind the door seeped out, already it had reached the Sasquatch's feet and blood merged there. The Sasquatch bawled out in a pain filled cry that rocked the night.

Porter was shook. What to do? Flee? He fought the dread panic that threatened to fill him to the core. That horrid jelly-like substance welled up from under the doorway. Probing tendrils slithered across the ground like venomous serpents.

"Come on son, you know what to do," called Mr. Nodens.

Each pounding on the door gave off an electrical sting, slightly shocking Porter every time he touched the metal. He didn't know how the Sasquatch could handle it. His hair and beard were standing on end and his scalp beneath his slouch hat prickled.

"Finish it!" shouted Nodens.

Porter grimaced at the old man, but he put both hands on the key, withstanding the arcing shocks, and turned it. The book spun in place, then sunk into the door. A bluish light gleamed like the noonday sun all about the edges.

The gelatinous snaking arms, now as large as pythons, froze and fell dead in puddles of goo, while the force banging against the door abruptly stopped.

"You did it son," said Mr. Nodens. "Always knew you had it in you."

Porter tore off his hat and held back the burning temptation to punch Nodens. "There's a whole lot you could have saved me the trouble on!"

Nodens chuckled. "I helped you out, but I didn't owe you anything, remember that. If you failed, these folks would have all failed with you. Be grateful you done good, but don't presume to know my business."

The Sasquatch seemed near as agitated as Porter, but it just stood huffing and giving a vengeful eye to Nodens.

"You know what to do, Jerahoe, get to it."

The Sasquatch turned and, with its massive hands, as big as spades themselves, began pulling down great heaps of the mountain and reburying the doorway.

Though Nodens appeared to be well over seventy years old, he was spry, and strode to the doorway, somehow always avoiding the Sasquatch's great handfuls of earth. He turned the lock on the door and pulled the key out.

"Can't just leave it in the lock, can we?" he said to no one in particular.

"Now what?" asked Porter.

"Now I put it somewhere safer than on the veritable doorstep. Ghost Horn's people knew not to go prying into these things, but your kind don't."

"My kind? It was Fei Buk."

Nodens held up a hand, brushing off Porter's excuses. "It was modern man that disturbed the cairn. If it hadn't been those Chinese fellers, it would have been another Forty-Niner in no time. No, I'll have to get this put in a special place where those that don't respect the sacred old times cannot find it."

The Sasquatch and the other Indians had a good-sized pile of earth over the top of the door. The Sasquatch even grabbed boulders of a size and weight Porter found unbelievable and wedged them over the top.

"That's good Jerahoe, you're done for now," said Nodens. "Go on home to Clarva and the kids."

"Kids?" puzzled Porter.

"Of course," said Nodens. "Everyone's got a family somewhere. Ain't nothing singular in this whole world. Closest thing I know to that singularity would be you, actually."

"Me?"

"Sure, blessed by a holy man that no bullet nor blade can harm you so long as you keep your hair long. That's mighty different. You just gotta watch your back." Nodens grinned and tipped his hat.

The Sasquatch breathed a sigh of relief and grunted something that sounded friendly at Ghost Horn, though he still gave the stink-eye to Nodens before trotting away into the tree line, leaving big bloody footprints behind.

Porter watched him go with a sense of awe. That such a huge thing could move so silently when it wished and vanish like that was astounding.

Ghost Horn and the other Indians seemed to be breathing a sigh of relief as well and moving back toward whatever was left of their village.

Nodens stood nearby, that half-smile on his face irritated Porter more with each passing second.

Mary held out a flask to Porter. "Thought you might want a drink now."

"You read my mind," he said. He was thinking of a cutting word for Nodens, something to really tell the man in no uncertain terms how he should carry himself to hell, but as he brought the flask down, there was no one standing there any longer. The mysterious old man was gone despite there being no where he could have possibly gone to that fast.

"Son of a gun," mused Porter. "Do we have anything to show for these last few days?"

"You are Big Medicine, you stopped the Old Ones from waking," she said stolidly.

"I don't know about that. I saw at least one open his eyes. They burned like molten iron."

Mary shook her head. "It is taken care of, they sleep or Nodens would not be gone."

"Yeah, but we spent a helluva lot of ammunition. We lost Zeke. Dawg lost his damn tail! What do we have to show for it all?"

"You worry too much about things."

Porter frowned at that. He had always considered himself frugal and of reasonable purpose and prospects.

She acknowledged his concern. "We have horses from Stoney's crew."

He nodded with a wry grin. "Yes we do. And considerably less pukes to deal with in the vicinity. Maybe that is a win I can talk about in the morning."

"You will not talk about the rest? The sacred mountain and Old Ones?"

Porter shook his shaggy head. "Hell no."

THE END FOR NOW...

If you enjoyed this kindly leave a review, that means the world to writers like me. Thanks for reading.

About the Author:

David J. West writes dark fantasy and weird westerns because the voices in his head won't quiet until someone else can hear them. He is a great fan of sword & sorcery, ghosts and lost ruins, so of course he lives in Utah in with his wife and children.

You can visit him online at:
https://david-j-west.blogspot.com/
https://twitter.com/David_JWest
Also check out other adventures with Porter in

the **DARK TRAILS SAGA** or the #SAVANT series.

Made in the USA
Coppell, TX
11 April 2020